RUSTLER'S CANYON

E.E. HALLERAN

WILDSIDE PRESS

1

One look at Latigo Pass was enough to tell Larry McCall that this was not the same little tank town he had known in the old days. Instead of the half dozen sheet-iron and adobe shacks clustered around the railroad's water tank, there was now a sizeable community with well-defined streets and a fair sprinkling of two-story buildings. Even the water tower was different.

McCall's greenish-gray eyes twinkled as he looked at the rust-streaked tank. Thought of the old wooden one brought back humorous memories and he let his thin lips quirk into a reminiscent grin. Then the lean, freckled countenance sobered once more as he glanced out across the sprawling railroad yard with its strings of ore cars waiting on multiple sidings. Beyond the neat depot he could see a well-traveled road leading through the mesquite into the border hills to the south. Latigo Pass had grown enormously, booming on the strength of the silver discoveries down there, and McCall knew an odd sense of unreality. He had come back to what was practically his home town but he was not finding very much that was familiar.

He fished papers and tobacco from the side pocket of the loose coat he wore, using the act of cigarette making to cover an adjustment of thoughts. Ever since taking this job he had been thinking of Latigo in terms of the little town he had once known; now he had to recognize that this was going to have unforeseen complications. He would have to start from scratch.

The westbound train that had brought him pulled away then and he felt a little better about it. Now he could see the rocky Wapitis frowning down upon the town from the north, guarding the barren pass like a medevial battlement. In that direction everything seemed unchanged. The town had not spread out to the north as it had done toward the south so the vista was the old familiar one of mesquite and alkali, merging into bare rock as the Wapitis reared their ragged heights out of the flatlands of the pass. Even the heat ripples over the mesquite seemed familiar. Latigo Pass had altered sharply in five years, but the Wapitis were the same forbidding old crags.

McCall bent his long length at the waist, groping half absently for the bulging carpetbag which lay at his feet. The little heat devils whirling in the powdery dust of Latigo's main street warned him that this was no day to stand out in the afternoon sun. Down here along the border most folks observed the Mexicans' siesta and it seemed clear that Latigo Pass was accepting the custom without reservation. Certainly the street was bare of people, and only two men had appeared on the station platform to meet the train. The siesta was smart business, McCall decided, particularly for a travel-weary pilgrim.

As he lifted his bag, however, he heard himself addressed by one of the two men he had noticed. Vaguely he had seen that the fellow was tremendously large, but it was only now that he noticed the shining star on the giant's open vest. There was an equally shiny pair of guns to go with the star and a fine black mustache that had been waxed to a sheen that rivaled the hardware. Otherwise the big man was a little on the unkempt side.

"Just a minute, stranger," the burly marshal said a little awkwardly. "I hope yo' won't take it amiss if I ask yo' a question or so." He was being carefully polite but he was not quite convincing with it. "I'm Ross Doyle, town marshal of Latigo Pass, and I make it a point to know who's comin' to town and why." There was a nervous grimness behind the words which McCall found hard to interpret. Asking strangers their business was a pretty ticklish proposition, but it did not appear that Marshal Doyle would be timid about such a matter. Still he was definitely uneasy.

McCall had to look up to meet the steady inquiry of the lawman's black eyes, a fact somewhat unusual in itself. Larry McCall did not have to look up to many men, but Marshal Ross Doyle must have towered a good six foot six. Even without guns a man of his bulk could do a lot toward keeping a town in order. McCall hoped he wouldn't find Doyle on the wrong side.

"Sounds reasonable enough," he told the big man easily, a little relieved that he could tell his story early and maybe save a lot of loose talk. "I'm Larry McCall and I used to live around here when this fine metropolis was just a pup. About five years ago I got itchy-footed and ran off to join a show. Lately I got a hankering to sashay back and see how the place managed to get along without me. Here I am—and it looks like my absence was just what the town needed."

The big man's attitude changed abruptly. "Yo're McCall, hey? Would yo' be the red-headed young hellion I've heard Shorty Langan lyin' about?"

McCall yanked off his Stetson to display the curly red thatch which had become so familiar to eastern vaudeville audiences. "There's the red," he told Doyle. "And I reckon I was kind of a hellion. But don't hold me accountable for any of Shorty Langan's yarns."

The big man was grinning amiably now, his nervousness gone. "Shorty's a right truthful gent when he ain't on the subject of Texas. I reckon he ain't done yo' no injustice. Yo're the feller what shot his initials in the railroad's water tank, ain't yo'?"

"So I'm famous," McCall chuckled. "A fine thing for a man to be remembered for!"

Doyle grinned again. "We heard the yarn when the railroad put up that new iron tank. They got tired o' havin' drunks climb up to pull the plugs outa yore bullet holes."

"I reckon I'd best keep shady," McCall said quizzically. "They might decide to bill me for a new tank."

"That part's none o' my business," the marshal told him, still smiling. "All I want is to keep the peace around here. Try to remember yo're full growed now. Likewise with Latigo. We got laws. No guns in town. No crooks, gamblers or gunmen. Yo' ain't totin' iron now, are yo'?"

"Not one on my person. Got a Colt in my bag."

"Keep it there and we'll git along fine." It was a friendly warning but a serious one.

McCall took it at face value. He knew that he might have sharp need for Marshal Doyle's support before this chore was over so he was well content to establish friendly relations. "What's your guess on a hotel, marshal?" he inquired. "Have you got one in Latigo that feeds reasonable and don't have too many head of livestock in the beds?"

Doyle chuckled. "Try the Silver Strike. It's no worse than the others, mebbe better'n most. They'll feed yo' plenty."

"Thanks. I'll try to be a model young man while I'm in Latigo Pass."

The big man laughed aloud and waved a huge paw. "That's a promise. I'll be around to ack right mean if'n yo' fergit it."

McCall nodded, tossed away the partly smoked cigarette, and picked up his bag. He didn't know just why he felt uneasy about this interview with the Latigo law, but somehow Ross Doyle didn't quite ring true. The man had been quite genial, even with his warning, but there was still a tense watchfulness about him which his bluff good humor could not quite hide. McCall could only hope that the watchfulness did not stem from a knowledge of the newcomer's errand. On a chore like

4

this one it didn't pay to share a secret with anyone, not even a lawman.

Sweat was running down his ribs and his shirt was sticking to his back when he entered the grubby front room of the Silver Strike Hotel. A chubby little man was asleep behind the rough pine desk, perspiration standing out in little globules on his smooth forehead. He was a total stranger but that was not surprising. Most of the inhabitants of Latigo Pass would be strangers, men who had come in on the tide of silver prosperity when the mine company turned the old water stop into a shipping point. McCall poked a thumb tentatively into the fat man's well-padded midriff and stated his wants without preliminary.

The man hauled himself to his feet and pointed to the stained daybook which served as a register. "Sign up," he instructed, putting on what seemed to be his idea of a businesslike air. "Are you plannin' to stay with us long?"

"Overnight. I've got a place back in the mountains."

"Prospect hole, you mean?"

"No. A ranch. I still own it although I haven't seen it for five years."

The round face twisted into a frown. "Which direction?" he asked, a note of concern creeping into his reedy voice. Then he seemed to catch himself for he added quickly, "None o' my business, of course, but there ain't many ranches in this dismal part of the territory and it seems funny to hear a man talk about ownin' one."

McCall shrugged. This was one line of questioning he had hoped to meet. It permitted him to explain himself and at the same time disclaim any interest in Latigo Pass. Still he was suspicious of the way the fat man had asked the question. The hotel keeper was not quite natural with his interest, just as Marshal Doyle had not been natural.

5

"The place is back in the Wapitis," he explained, watching the fat man's expression. "I lived there with my father until he died. Then I rented the place and went wandering."

The broad face had gone blank but there was a note of concern in the piping voice as the hotel man asked, "You mean Jim Tanner's place?"

"Tanner was the name of the tenant. A share and share alike proposition."

Suddenly the fat man laughed. "I'll bet you've been getting a bright lot of share outa that place! Old Tanner can't even pay his one hired man, they tell me."

"That's why I'm here," McCall said quietly, trying to understand the fellow's real meaning. "It seems as though the place ought to do well enough—but it sure hasn't been doing it."

"Poor land and a poor manager," the fat man stated. "You can't make much outa them rocks, and Jim Tanner ain't the man to do miracles. Just a blundering old fool, they tell me. I ain't seen him in a year."

A new voice broke into the conversation sharply. "That is quite enough gossip, Father!"

McCall looked up to see a tall girl standing in the doorway behind the desk. Her features were good enough to be interesting, even with the present frown, while her chestnut hair was worn in a neat braid that softened the somewhat angular lines of her face. A soiled apron hinted that she did a full share of work around the Silver Strike even though she did presume to speak sharply to the proprietor.

"My fault," McCall said promptly. "I asked for information and got it."

She eyed him without expression for a second or two, then turned away and disappeared. The fat man chuckled uneasily. "Daisy's mighty tart sometimes. Livin' in a frontier town seems to make women that way. They get afraid to open their mouths for fear

6

they'll stir up trouble." He put on an elaborate laugh that had entirely too much worry in it as he added, "Mebbe that's a good thing in a way. Most women talk too much. Come along and I'll show you a room."

He talked volubly as he led the way up a bare staircase that smelled of alkali dust, stale cooking and green lumber. In a space of about a minute and a half he covered the weather, the probable effect of the coming election on silver prices, and the betting on Cleveland to win. Not once did he make any other reference to McCall's errand in town. Evidently he was heeding his daughter's warning.

McCall glanced at the room and nodded his acceptance. The fat man said, "Supper in about two hours," and hurried away.

McCall watched him thoughtfully as he disappeared down the stairs, then he went into the room and closed the door. So far he had met three people in Latigo Pass and all three of them had behaved in a rather unusual manner. The whole trouble was that there seemed to be no hint of a pattern in that odd behavior. Doyle had been uneasy until the newcomer was identified, but the hotel man had displayed no uneasiness until after such identification. Maybe that was the pattern.

He had counted heavily on his own reputation to help him in his work here. People might remember him, as Doyle had done, for his youthful antics around Latigo Pass or they might know something of his career in show business. Either way they would accept him as a harmless addition to the local scene. His true identity would link him with the Wapiti region instead of the silver mine area to the south where his real errand seemed to center. All things considered it had looked like a smart plan to play himself—but now he was not so sure. Matters were shaping up in a fashion he did not like.

He crossed to the open window, intending to shut out some of the heat by drawing the flimsy shade, but he

7

pulled up short at sight of a pudgy figure hurrying along in the dusty heat toward the depot. It seemed like a peculiar time for the fat hotel man to be displaying so much energy but there he was, almost running.

The false front of the adjoining building blocked him out for a moment or two but he emerged on the other side where McCall could witness his meeting with Marshal Ross Doyle. Judging by the quick gestures of the fat man he was reporting the arrival of Larry McCall, reporting it with a nervous energy which hinted at some concern. Doyle seemed uninterested at first but then his attitude changed abruptly and the two men went into a brisk conference. The talk lasted for several minutes before Doyle turned away hurriedly, leaving the hotel man to hasten back to the Silver Strike.

McCall knew that his vague uneasiness had been well founded but he still could not understand what the fuss was about. What had he said to the hotel man that could have produced so much excitement? He had been equally frank with Doyle and the marshal had shown no sign of special interest. It didn't make sense.

He stretched himself wearily on the lumpy cot, giving up the prospective siesta in favor of some serious thinking. His arrival in Latigo Pass had been conducted with careful casualness and he had found two quick opportunities to let people know that he was not interested in the growing town. That should have been good strategy but in some fashion it seemed to be back-firing. That fat man downstairs had picked up a quick suspicion. McCall could not believe that his one brief fling as a range detective would be known to the hotel keeper. Nor could there have been a leak from headquarters of the Apache Mining Company. Even their local manager was not to be informed of McCall's errand in Latigo.

He was still thoughtful and completely perplexed when he answered the first bell for supper. The fat man was not in sight on the lower floor but already there was a brisk clash of crockery from what appeared to be the dining room. McCall went toward it, aware that a thin, rather colorless man of slender build was following him. He had an impression that the thin man had been lounging near the door, apparently waiting for him. That seemed logical enough. Some sort of spy would be on his trail every minute from now on.

He found a seat at one of the two long tables in the hot room, making a hasty appraisal of two early diners as he sat down. One of them was a dark-faced, squatty looking hombre in nondescript garments while the other was clean-shaven, alert looking and unusually well dressed. McCall checked this second man's angular features in a swift mental inventory. Long nose, brown eyes, receding hair line, small mustache and pointed chin. Along with the well-tailored garments that added up to Gordon Stallcup, local manager for the Apache Mining Company. Stallcup was the man who had reported the odd happenings around Latigo and the mines. Presumably he would be the man to trust if the case should develop to the point where McCall needed help. He seemed intelligent enough but he didn't look like much of a fighter, McCall thought.

Stallcup nodded an easy greeting but possible conversation was interrupted by the entrance of the young woman McCall had seen before. She was wearing a clean apron now but otherwise she seemed much as she had been before, quite neat, reasonably attractive and forbiddingly stern.

"All we've got is steak," she announced abruptly. "Want that?"

"Bring it on," McCall assented. "A steak to eat, another steak to sop up the gravy and a third one for dessert."

"Don't get fresh or that's just what you'll have. Otherwise there's bread, tomatoes and apple pie."

"I'm meek. Make it one steak a big one."

9

She disappeared into the noisy kitchen just as another diner bustled into the room. The newcomer's loud greeting caused something of a stir and McCall looked up to see a big man in a check suit that might have been more appropriate to an eastern race track. The breezy one was not out of his thirties but he was showing signs of a stomach and double chin. The gray streaked hair was plastered carefully over a small bald spot while the military mustache was trimmed meticulously. In thirty seconds of rapid fire talk he convinced McCall that the racetrack suit was no disguise. The man fitted the garments.

He greeted Stallcup with some little restraint but boomed jovial salutations at the other two. McCall learned that the thin man was named Jones while the dark, stocky one was Zellers. Then the loud one bustled across to McCall.

"Stranger in town, aren't you, brother? Welcome to our fine little city. My name is Henderson Ott and I run the land office here. Stop around and see me if you're interested in locating where values are bound to increase. Stop and see me anyway. No charge." He laughed loudly at his own joke and extended a well-tended hand. "What's for dinner?"

"McCall's the name," Larry said, taking the hand. "And it's steak."

The noisy one blinked. "What? Oh, steak. You mean for supper. I didn't follow you for a second. Steak, eh?" He let his booming laugh fill the room again. "Don't we always have steak? And why not? Best steaks in the southwest, and the cheapest. Eh, boys?"

His heavy humor aroused scant enthusiasm. Stallcup did not even look around and, after a flat silence, the swarthy Zellers growled, "Why don't yuh shut up, Ott? That tongue o' yores runs too dam' much."

The re-entry of Daisy interrupted what had the makings of a sharp exchange of words and Ott transferred his breezy attentions to the girl. It left McCall to the realization that he had learned one thing about Latigo Pass. The reference to cheap beef meant a well-known cattle rustling business. It did not seem to have much connection with the troubles which had caused the Apache Mining Company to send him down here, but he stored the information away for future use. A man never knew when a fact would come in handy.

By the time the meal was over he had added a few more facts to his store. He knew that Zellers had a marked dislike for Henderson Ott. He suspected that Ott might be making passes at Daisy. He had a further suspicion that the girl might be receptive to the idea. At any rate she had left her work in the dining room, turning the chores over to an older woman with a remark about getting dressed. However, he decided that there was another point of more importance to be noted, the fact that Zellers was obviously not accustomed to dining at the Silver Strike. The meal was almost over before McCall realized it, and then he noticed only because of the way the man was killing time. Jones was not the only spy who had been set to watch the newcomer in Latigo Pass; the dark-featured Zellers was on the same errand.

It gave McCall something to think about as he went out into the front hall of the hotel. One spy would have been disconcerting enough but two spies hinted at a complication he had not foreseen. He was inclined to be a little rueful about the whole thing. Just when he had been congratulating himself on making a perfect entry into town he found himself under the surveillance of two different parties. It was not very flattering to a man who thought himself reasonably smart—and it was not comfortable. People who had to set spies on strangers· probably would not be backward about using stronger measures.

2

McCall saw that Ott had stopped near the front door, talking in low tones to a notably changed Daisy. The girl had dressed quickly. Her white shirtwaist and neat skirt were not flashy but they set off her well-rounded figure to good advantage. Certainly Ott seemed to be impressed for he had reached out to put an arm around her, pulling her toward him in defiance of her sharp protest.

McCall started toward the darkening street, curious to see what his two shadows would do now. As he was reaching for the door, however, he heard the girl's voice raised in quick anger. He looked around, saw that both Jones and Zellers were retreating into the dining room, and caught Daisy's glance of entreaty.

"Something wrong?" he inquired, keeping his voice casual.

Her lips opened as though to reply but Ott put a hand over her mouth. He was putting on his show of boisterous good humor but there was something hard beneath the mannerism as he replied, " She likes to be coaxed, brother. Better trot along."

McCall hesitated. The girl's quick change of clothing had certainly been for some purpose and it might be that this was just a part of her act. Maybe she had set out to attract Ott and was now playing coy. It didn't always pay to take a woman's protests at face value. Still he didn't like the fellow's sneering attitude.

It was the girl's move that helped him to a decision. She tore herself away from Ott and aimed a blow at his face. It was not a slap but a solid punch such as a man might have thrown. Ott took it, rocked with the force of it, and closed in again, mauling her as anger overcame his earlier emotion. Then McCall took a hand.

He clamped a firm fist on the land agent's collar and heaved, hauling the man halfway across the room and forcing him to release the girl. "She don't want to be coaxed that much," he said calmly. "Go peddle some town lots and behave yourself."

Ott's face went scarlet as he twisted around to aim a swing at McCall. "Want trouble, do you?" he snarled. "I'll . . ."

McCall never learned what his opponent's intentions were. He caught the blow, gripping Ott's wrist in a practiced fist. Then he whirled swiftly and heaved the angry man bodily over his shoulder. Ott landed heavily, cursing as he struggled to right himself. McCall followed up his advantage, however, catching the fellow by the collar again before he could rise. One heave brought Ott to his feet and a second one propelled him forcibly through the door and into the deepening twilight. It all happened so swiftly and with such apparent ease that it drew a little gasp from the watching girl.

"Sorry if I chased away a customer," he told her. "But maybe he'll come back if he likes the steaks as much as he said he did."

She looked a little uncomfortable at the mention of steaks but her voice was steady as she murmured, "Thanks. I'm sorry if I've caused you any trouble."

"No trouble at all."

"He won't forget it, you know."

"I hope not."

There was a flat silence and then Jones and Zellers came out of the dining room once more, crossing toward the still open front door. Zellers paused to grin crookedly at the girl. "I reckon yuh won't need no more help, Daisy," he observed, putting an odd emphasis on the words.

She seemed to understand something which was a mystery to McCall for she replied in much the same tone. "I think everything is under control now, Jake. You won't need to bother."

Again McCall knew that feeling of bafflement. These two were talking about something other than the recent fracas, something which might mean a lot to him. Maybe Daisy was a part of the queer little plot which had developed so suddenly after his arrival at the Silver Strike.

He watched her narrowly as they were left alone, in the room. It seemed clear that she was trying to apply herself to some sort of effort for she stood silent, clenching and unclenching her hands nervously. Suddenly she looked up, putting on a smile that had plenty of charm in it.

"Maybe you'd do well to stay off the street this evening, Mr. McCall. Ott has friends in town, you know."

"Is that a warning or an invitation?"

"Maybe it's both."

He met her eyes squarely and proceeded to build a smoke. She watched without speaking and he knew that she was waiting rather anxiously for his reply. Too anxiously, he decided, for the apparent casualness of the occasion.

"I'll probably never get a cuter hint," he said with calm deliberation, "but I've got to ride into the hills at daybreak so I'll need to make my arrangements this evening."

She flushed a little but continued to meet his scrutiny. "What's so inviting about hills? Put the trip off for a day or so. The hills will still be there." She tried to make it sound flippant but he caught the hint of strain, much the same note he had spotted in her brief exchange with Zellers.

"Sorry," he said, meaning it just a little. "I'm afraid I'd better stick to my plans. When a pretty gal gets a fellow playing the *mañana* game he's a dead duck."

She turned away abruptly and he watched her disappear through the doorway behind the desk. There was a grim smile on his lips as he clapped the Stetson down hard on the red head and strode toward the door. So that was the way this game was going to be played!

He walked slowly away from the hotel, then crossed the street and stood in the shadow of an unlighted building. He had not been able to figure out any good reason why Daisy had been set to the task of keeping him in Latigo Pass but he was dead sure that such had been the reason for her recent moves. Everything pointed to that conclusion even if it did sound crazy.

He did not have long to wait. Daisy came out of the Silver Strike almost at a run, hurrying away toward the south end of town. Reporting failure, McCall decided. Probably something of an embarrassment for her after the way she had dismissed the efficient Mr. Zellers. McCall thought of following her but decided against it. Time enough to take action when he was sure of his ground. Meanwhile he would seize the opportunity to visit Shorty Langan while he was not subject to a bit of guarding.

There were few stores along the north side of town but even after he had crossed the railroad line McCall could sense the uneasiness of the community. Some men laughed but others restrained themselves uneasily. Some gossiped loudly while others whispered in corners. A part of Latigo Pass seemed to be bursting with the normal energy of a young town while another part was sullenly watchful. McCall could only guess that the trouble was connected with the mission which had brought him to town. And maybe the guess was all wrong. These folks might simply have guilty knowledge of the rustling activities which had been mentioned at the hotel. Or they might just be restless under the harsh rule of a tough lawman.

He paused twice, making sure that no one was trailing him. He was grinning a little when he stopped in front of a rambling adobe livery stable. That business with Daisy had put the guards completely out of business.

Then he caught a flicker of movement in a shadow near the railroad tracks. Damn! He had congratulated himself too soon. Someone had picked up the trail already. Now he would have to alter his plans for talking with Langan, at least to the extent of allowing for an eavesdropper.

He stood silently for a moment or two, spelling out the big sign which was barely readable in the lights from the nearer buildings. LANGAN'S LONE STAR LIVERY. The legend brought a chuckle. Shorty Langan's place had been a landmark in Latigo Pass ever since there had been the beginnings of a town there. Evidently the building had been enlarged to suit the needs of the larger community but the sign was the same. Shorty Langan would never forget his boasted Texas origin.

A swinging lantern just inside the open door provided enough light for him to recognize the slight figure of his old friend, but it took Langan several seconds to realize who his visitor was. Then the stableman came forward with a yell, pounding McCall on the back and pumping his hand energetically.

"Where in tunket have ye been, Larry, ye red-headed rascal? Last I heard of ye was when ye wrote that ye was joinin' a circus or somethin'."

"That's the answer," McCall told him, meeting the firm handclasp. "With a circus or somethin'. I did gun tricks, some fancy ropin' and maybe a bit of ridin'. Sometimes it was with a circus, but in winter it was stage stuff. I was a pretty fancy hairpin, I'll tell you."

The little man sniffed disdainfully. "Never thought ye'd ever go in fer dude stuff, Larry."

McCall laughed. "I'm properly ashamed. But it was good fun for a while."

"Ye mean ye've quit it?"

16

"Yep." McCall had been listening ever since coming into the stable and he knew now that the watcher was posted outside. He made his next statement carefully, knowing that its effect might be a double one. "I'm just not the actor type, I reckon. I got mighty restless showin' off in front of greenhorns all the time. That's why I rambled back here to see what Jim Tanner has been doing with K-Bar. I'd kinda like to fork an honest cow pony for a change after bein' on show horses so much. What have you got that I can hire for a day or so? I want to ride out and see Tanner."

He watched narrowly to check the effect of the words on Langan. Other folks in Latigo Pass had shown marked interest in his plans for riding into the Wapitis, and he had been half afraid that Langan would act the same way. The little man merely nodded, apparently taking the idea as a casual one.

"I got most any kind o' nag ye might want, Larry. I don't reckon, though, that ye'll git much fun outa seein' Tanner. He ain't had much luck with K-Bar, I hear."

"What's wrong?"

"I dunno. Never see Tanner around Latigo any more since he started dealin' over at Mesa. I did hear that he'd lost stock, and I remember that his wife died a year or two ago. Jest an unlucky feller, I suppose."

"Is he running the place alone?"

"Got one hired hand, I reckon. And that spraddle-laigged gal o' his'n. Mebbe she's big enough to be some help by now."

"Sounds to me like K-Bar needs somebody to take care of things. Set me up a complete outfit for to-morrow morning, Shorty. I'll be riding out at daylight."

Langan stared. "Ye ain't figurin' to take a hand in the business again, are ye?"

"Maybe. There's worse things than having a good cow outfit close to a growing town like Latigo Pass. A man could make some nice money without too much shipping trouble."

"Gosh, I didn't figure ye'd want any more ranchin'. It's a heap harder work than puttin' on shows."

"That's the way I felt about it five years ago. Now I'm a bit fed up with show business. Getting back to something real wouldn't be so doggone bad, I guess." He had been talking for the ears of that fellow who had been standing just outside the doorway, but suddenly he knew that the words sounded pretty good in his own ears. Maybe his own restlessness had been an urge to get back on the range. Show business had ceased to hold its charm and this range detective game hadn't turned out to be all he had expected it to be. Maybe he ought to think seriously about K-Bar. After he cleaned up the job for the mining company, of course.

Langan was suddenly voluble, talking about prospects in the region of Latigo Pass. McCall let him talk, busy with his own thoughts and at the same time keeping an ear attuned to the occasional rustle which betrayed the presence of the spy outside. Knowledge that the watcher must be uncomfortable out there made McCall prolong the interview, encouraging Langan to gossip endlessly about all sorts of petty subjects. The talk might not help to divert attention from him, marking him as harmless, but at least it would make the spy earn his hire.

It was pretty late when he broke off the conversation and announced his intention of getting some sleep. By that time it had been agreed that Langan would provide a pony, bedroll, and a complete outfit for the morning. Also the guard had gone away. McCall had heard the fellow's stealthy withdrawal and had strolled to the stable door, watching in the darkness until he caught sight of a slender figure passing a lighted window. It seemed pretty clear that the man who had been outside the livery stable was the colorless fellow who had been called Jones at the hotel. Evidently he had not let himself be thrown off guard by Daisy. And maybe that meant something. Daisy and Zellers could be working for one outfit while Jones could represent another. With so many cross currents becoming apparent it seemed likely that there was more than one force operating in Latigo Pass.

McCall was trying to make more sense out of that idea when he left the stable, and his preoccupation made him a little unwary. As a result he was caught completely off guard when a big man lurched out of the shadows to aim a heavy blow at his head. In the darkness he knew only that he was being attacked so he reacted swiftly, shaking off the first stunning blow as he wheeled to defend himself. His assailant grunted, evidently disappointed at the failure to down McCall at the first rush, then he came in again. McCall saw him for just an instant against a distant window, the silhouette telling him several things about the man. Then he was sidestepping a second rush and driving a solid punch to the stranger's bull neck. It was becoming clear that the man was not much of a fighter at this sort of game.

By that time McCall knew that he was dealing with a cowboy rather than a miner and the information pleased him. Miners might brawl with fists but cowpunchers were notoriously averse to any kind of fight which did not involve a gun. Even a big man like this one could be handled by a fellow who knew his business.

McCall was even smiling a little as he watched his man turn for a third assault. He feinted, drew a wild swing, and stepped in to drive a hard right to the pit of the big man's stomach. It brought an agonized grunt and as the man doubled up, McCall threw in successive rights and lefts which knocked the enemy completely off his feet. The fellow was too tough for a knockout, however, and he rolled quickly, taking to his heels and disappearing behind the nearest building. McCall let him go.

The scuffle did not seem to have attracted any notice so McCall stood motionless for a few seconds, trying to decide whether any other action was to be expected. Then he moved across the tracks toward the Silver Strike, frowning perplexedly as he tried to guess a reason fòr this attack. He had assumed that the meek looking spy had been following him for information purposes. That part made sense, especially after the earlier events of the evening. But how would the spying be connected with an unprovoked attack? An attempted murder might have indicated that the enemy was aware of his true errand but a mere slugging bout did not make sense. There was always the chance that this had been simply an attempted robbery, but McCall was not ready to believe it.

His proposed ride out to the K-Bar spread now loomed as distinctly significant. Originally he had planned the trip as a blind, resenting the delay involved but figuring that it would establish his harmlessness in the minds of this mysterious crowd that seemed to be operating out of Latigo Pass. Now it was becoming clear that he had stumbled into something. They didn't want him to go. Which made the journey a prime necessity. He had to go—and he had to go without letting the enemy know why he was going.

He left the street a hundred yards short of the hotel, entering a general store which was still open for business. Shorty Langan would provide a complete trail outfit but McCall wanted an extra shirt. A man never went wrong having a spare shirt in his slicker roll. A toothless little man waited on him promptly and conversationally, praising the quality of the garment even after McCall was heading through the door with the bundle under his arm.

He had taken no more than a dozen steps, merely

clearing the corner of the building, when something moved in the darkness of the side alley. McCall started to turn but a voice interrupted the movement, a harsh voice which seemed vaguely familiar.

"Stand hard there! Drop the bundle and put yuhr paws up!" A hard object bored into his back to enforce the command.

McCall obeyed, impressed both by the hard object and by the cold edge of decision in the unknown's low voice. He still did not know any good reason why he should be the object of so much uncomfortable attention but he was certainly getting it. And this time it had a pretty deadly ring to it. Feminine wiles and physical strength had failed; now the enemy had turned to guns.

"The marshal won't like it if he catches you playing with firearms," McCall said, sparring for time.

"Shut up! Back up here into the shadow! I ain't keen on havin' yuh attract attention."

McCall backed, the gun muzzle digging into his ribs as though the gunman wanted to warn him against any break. A hasty glance along the street had told him that no one was within noticing distance; there wasn't much to be done except to obey orders and hope for the best.

3

Two backward steps took McCall out of the dim light which the street provided but as he moved he turned the upper half of his body a little, looking back over his shoulder to address the gunman in a mildly complaining voice. "What's the idea, mister? Ain't you mistaking me for somebody else?"

"No mistakes, pilgrim! I ain't . . ."

That was as far as he went. McCall completed his body twist in the split second of mental distraction that went with the talk. At the same time he brought his right elbow down and around in a vicious arc that swept the gun clear of his body. The swift pivot also brought his left hand through in a hard left hook which caught the gunman flush on the mouth. There was a sharp smack as fist met chin and a louder sound as the gun exploded harmlessly past McCall's side. Almost as quickly the holdup man was flat on his back.

McCall wasted no time in sentiment. He flung himself upon his antagonist, wrenching the gun loose and bringing its butt hard against the side of the fallen gunman's head. Only then did he realize why the fellow's voice had seemed familiar. This was Jake Zellers, the swarthy gent who had done guard duty at suppertime. This crazy game was getting more and more complicated all the time.

He clambered to his feet as running footsteps sounded from two directions. Apparently the sound of a gunshot in Latigo Pass was sufficiently unusual to attract quick attention. McCall moved deliberately into the light but before he could answer a single question he saw the towering form of Marshal Ross Doyle at his elbow. The lawman had been mighty prompt to arrive.

"What's goin' on here?" Doyle barked. "Who done the shootin'?"

McCall motioned with the gun toward the prone figure in the shadow. "That jasper tried to . . ."

"It's you, hey?" Doyle interrupted. "Didn't I warn yuh not to tote iron in this town? Dammit, man, I'll . . ."

"Wait a minute. I wasn't carrying the gun and nobody got shot. This waddie stuck it in my ribs and I took it away from him. Here. Take it." He shoved the weapon into the marshal's big fist. "I didn't want any part of it in the first place and I still don't—even when it's no longer pushed into my hind ribs."

Doyle laughed with open scorn. "Yuh ain't tellin' us

yuh took a gun away from a jigger what had yuh foul from behind, are yuh?"

"Wake him up and ask him. He probably won't be too sure what happened, but he'll know he lost his gun."

"Yeah? How do we know he did? Mebbe this is jest a yarn yuh're slinging us. Mebbe yuh had the gun all the time."

A new voice broke in then, that of the little storekeeper. "I'll tell ye that, Ross. This feller was jest in to buy hisself a shirt. I seen him tryin' it on and I'll swear he wasn't packin' a gun, outside or inside."

Doyle hesitated. Then he reacted to the murmur of belief which came from the crowd. "I reckon yuh oughta know, Abe. Here, somebody help me with this jigger. What'd yuh do to him, McCall?"

"Just combed his hair lightly with his gun butt. In case you want to know, he's a gent named Zellers. Don't ask me why he tried to stick me up; I don't know."

Doyle accepted the statement with surprising calmness, merely muttering an order to a couple of men who had edged into the alley with him. "Take his feet, Wells. Me and Tim will handle his shoulders. We'll drag him over to the calaboose and see what he's got to say fer hisself." He turned then, facing McCall as though just remembering his duty. "Stick around, McCall. Maybe he'll check yore yarn, and then again maybe he won't."

"You know where to find me," McCall said shortly. He was thinking that Ross Doyle had taken the incident in a curiously easy manner, almost as though he had expected something of the sort. The lawman had not even asked the identity of the man on the ground—and he had not been surprised when McCall volunteered the information.

It took a few minutes to get rid of the curious crowd but McCall slipped away as soon as possible, more than a little annoyed at the attention he had been attracting. It would have been much better to have left Latigo Pass as inconspicuously as possible but now that was out of the question. The only consolation was the probable fact that Doyle was equally disturbed by the publicity. Which was a point worth remembering.

He went to his room to leave the new shirt, taking time to do some fast thinking before returning to the lower floor. In some ways the evening had been significant, but in other ways it didn't make any sense at all. Someone had been making a persistent effort to get at him but the nature of the attacks had been a little ridiculous. A bushwhack bullet might have meant that his game in Latigo Pass was known; two clumsy attempts and the amiable effort of Daisy left him puzzled.

It was also leaving him jumpy, he discovered, when he stepped out into the gloomy hall and found a silent shadow beside him. He whirled to defend himself but brought up sharply as a feminine voice came softly: "Take it easy, mister. I won't hurt you." In the dim light coming up the stairway he saw that it was Daisy. The girl was still wearing the shirtwaist and skirt which he had seen earlier and he had the impression that she had just returned to the hotel.

"I'm getting so I don't take chances," he told her shortly. "When a man's been ambushed twice in an hour he gets kinda spooky."

"I don't blame you. That's why I came along. Would you take a bit of good advice?"

"I'd take it—but I wouldn't promise to follow it."

"Don't leave Latigo Pass." Her voice had dropped to a whisper and McCall couldn't tell whether it was merely a theatrical gesture or a sign that she was being careful.

"That's queer advice," he commented. "As soon as I hit town folks start throwing guns and fists at me, and you think I ought to stick around. How come?"

"I've said too much already. I can't tell you any more. But don't ride into the Wapitis."

.24

She turned and hurried down the stairs, leaving him to the thought that her final words had been quite illuminating. It helped him to accept a theory which had been running through his mind ever since Daisy's father rushed out to hold that sudden conference with Ross Doyle. The gentle attentions he had been receiving since that time were all based on one item the hotel man had known which had not been made clear to Doyle. It was the fact that Larry McCall proposed to ride out to K-Bar. McCall in Latigo was no worry to anyone; McCall on the trail through the Wapitis seemed to disturb a lot of people.

He was still turning the idea over in his mind when he went down to meet the returning marshal. Doyle had a ready explanation for the affair he had been handling. "Just a down-and-outer," he said easily. "Feller was broke and needin' a drink so he tried to stick up the first hombre what looked halfway prosperous. He admits it."

"That seems funny," McCall said. "I'm sure it was the same man who ate here at the hotel this evening. He didn't act like a grub line rider then."

Doyle laughed, a little uneasily. "Lots of hombres put on a good front 'til they're down to their last cent. I know this jigger and he's kinda that way. No real harm in him, I reckon, but I'll keep him on ice fer a spell."

The lawman was patently uneasy and McCall watched him curiously as he left the hotel. He would have offered pretty steep odds that the marshal had known about those attacks even before they were made. He gave Doyle a little time to get away from the Silver Strike, then he went up to his room and shucked out of his now familiar garments. Dungarees, a dark blue flannel shirt and a battered old sombrero would make him less conspicuous. As an added precaution he slipped out by way of a side door, emerging in a dark lane from which he could stroll idly into the street. Somewhat to his surprise he did not see any sign of a guard on duty.

There were few people on the streets now and he found it easy to loaf along, waiting for a dash of conversation which might be worth the overhearing. Finally he caught up with something that sounded interesting. From a saloon came the sound of a lively discussion and he leaned against a shadowed corner post to listen.

"I still think it was a frame-up," a nasal voice was insisting. "I seen that hombre on the ground before Doyle hauled him away and it was Jake Zellers, right enough. Jake ain't the waddie to git picked on by no greenhorn. When Jake throws down on a man it's no foolin'!"

"McCall's no greenhorn," someone else replied. "They say he used to live around here and was a tough enough button. Anway, it ain't good sense to figure that Jake got hisself slugged on purpose."

"How do ye know he was slugged? Mebbe it was all a fake."

"Why?"

"I dunno. I'm just wonderin'."

A third man cut in. "Yuh heard what Wells said, didn't yuh, Mace? Jake was slugged, all right. He was plumb flabbergasted when he woke up and found out what happened to him. He ain't sure yet how the tenderfoot sprung it on him."

"That was Wells' story," the nasal voice scoffed. "And who's Wells? Just a jigger what showed up here in Latigo less than a month back. Mebbe he's connected with whatever kind of a deal this is. Anyway it's plenty fishy to me."

"But what the hell could it mean?"

"Don't ask me. There's a heap o' things happenin' in Latigo that I don't know about."

The remark seemed to sound an ominous note, for the uneasy silence which followed it was accompanied by the scuffling of several pairs of bootheels. Then two men came toward the door and McCall set himself in motion, acting as though he were a casual passerby. He had heard enough to satisfy himself of a couple of points and it seemed clear that the men in the saloon knew no more.

He walked on thoughtfully, keeping an alert eye on the street and an ear cocked for the talk which drifted to him from behind the batwings. Most of Latigo was behind him when he spotted a familiar figure ahead. It was not likely that Latigo Pass boasted two men of such immense size so McCall faded into the shadows and advanced cautiously. The marshal crossed the street almost at once and went into a building which McCall decided was the local calaboose. The place was dark and Doyle did not strike a light. For a minute or so McCall expected to see the burly shadow returning to the street but instead there was another flicker of movement in the darkness. A second man emerged from somewhere and slipped quietly into the building. That seemed like hint enough. McCall went into action promptly, angling for an open space which would permit him to scout the building.

He saw quickly enough that he had picked the wrong side of the structure. There was the subdued rumble of Doyle's heavy voice and the crisper tones of another man swearing angrily. McCall had to circle behind the place, moving cautiously in order to avoid noise, and by the time he could take position under the window which showed a faint gleam of light he knew that Doyle had already done most of his talking. Certainly the other man's words seemed to be in the nature of a reply.

"The hell with that, Ross! If we can't keep him in town without stirring up a stink we'll have to play it some other way. We've gone to a lot of trouble to make Latigo what it is and we're not going to spoil our show front now. Too much attention is just what we don't want."

"But we can't let him . . ."

"You're borrowing trouble. It's a hundred to one he'll never notice anything."

"I'd like a hunk o' that bet," Doyle growled. "This jigger's sharp. He threw Hen Ott around like a rag-baby and he beat hell outa Ears Trondell. Yuh already know what happened to Jake."

The unknown laughed. "I'd like to have seen Ott get it. That windbag needs a good licking. Well, we'll agree that you've got a tough hombre on your hands. That's still no reason to start a riot in Latigo. Get a man on the trail right away and have him do a careful job of trail blotting out there in the Devil's Cockpit. That will be plenty."

"But suppose McCall . . . ?"

"Suppose nothing! The easy way is the smart way. I've told you a hundred times that we're going to play it cagy but you always want to throw your weight around. You and that fool Jake!"

"It looked like the only way," Doyle grumbled. "The jigger didn't go fer Daisy's act."

"And don't send Jake on the trail blotting job," the other man cut in. "For one thing you'll have to keep him in jail for a day or so just to make it look right. Anyway we need somebody with horse sense out there. By the way, are you sure this McCall jasper is what he makes out to be?"

"Dead certain. Shorty Langan knows him from when he used to live back there behind the Wapitis."

"Can you trust Langan?"

"No. But he ain't got any reason to lie to us on that. Anyway, he just told us what we already knew."

"Then we won't borrow trouble. Get a man started for the canyon right away. Tell him there's to be no gun play unless it's forced on him."

"Anybody partickler you want me to use?"

"Who's handy?"

"Olson's in town. Then there's the new man, Wells. Trondell has already headed back to his outfit."

"Send Olson. Tell him to mount guard out there until we know for sure where we stand with this pest. No shooting unless he sees that McCall is getting too smart. Then he's to make it a quick job—and one that nobody will ever find out about."

"Right."

"That's all. Better get moving. Remember, we don't want to draw attention and we don't want any fighting here in Latigo!"

McCall slipped away as the two men moved toward the front of the building. He watched while they moved out into the dark street, planning to make some attempt to identify the unknown man who was giving such snappy orders to the marshal. The plan was interrupted, however, as a foot scraped in the darkness at the rear of the calaboose. Someone else had been doing some scouting of the Latigo Pass jail tonight.

McCall started toward the sound but the other man was smart. Having made one betraying sound he gave up all attempts at stealthiness and fled. McCall heard him blundering into what sounded like a pile of packing boxes but he did not try to follow. There were other things more important to do.

He turned toward the street again, thinking hard as he ran. That other man must have been watching all the time yet he had given no alarm even though he must have known that McCall was listening to the talk between Doyle and the unknown boss. So he could not be one of Doyle's gang. Once again McCall felt certain that this crazy mess was more complicated than it had appeared.

When he reached the street Doyle and his companion were nowhere in sight. McCall edged his way along cautiously hoping to pick up the trail again but they had disappeared completely. Twice he turned into side lanes, cutting back sharply in an effort to trap anyone who might be tailing him but never was there any sign of surveillance. He saw nothing out of the way until he was at the door of the Silver Strike. Then he came face to face with the colorless little man who had watched him at supper and who had listened so long at the door of Langan's stable. The fellow still looked harmless but the knees of his pants were dusty and there was a gaping rip in the sleeve of his shirt.

McCall grinned amiably at him. "Rough night, partner," he observed. "A man gets all banged up tearing around in the dark—didn't you?"

The man turned away without replying.

Alone in his uncomfortable hot room McCall tried to sum up the things he had learned during the hectic evening. Marshal Ross Doyle was the front man for some kind of a gang which was operating out of Latigo Pass using the town's vaunted respectability for a mask. The swarthy Jake Zellers was a member of the gang and so was a man named Wells. McCall had no clear recollection of Wells's appearance, but he knew that he would be able to spot Trondell if he should meet him again. "Ears" Trondell, Doyle had called him. McCall remembered the silhouette he had seen when he was beating off the sudden attack and the memory brought a quizzical smile.

Olson was still just a name but McCall thought he knew what to expect there. Which was more than he could say for some other parts of the puzzle. Just how far was the fat hotel man implicated? And Daisy? The girl's part had been a little contradictory. She had made the first effort to keep him in Latigo Pass but she had gone out of her way to pass him a word of warning.

Henderson Ott was as much a mystery. The land agent had been mentioned by Doyle, but the reference had not made it clear that Ott was a member of the gang. And then there was the pale little man who had popped up so frequently during the evening. What was his game and where did he stand with Doyle? McCall knew that he would have to pick up a lot of answers and pick them up quickly. It was already clear that he had a formidable enemy to buck. And he didn't propose to fight in the dark if he could help it.

4

A few hours of sleep did nothing to dispel the grim realization that this was going to be a tough job. When McCall slid out of his cot in the early dawn he felt jittery, conscious that he had slept little and badly. His mind had been too active with the problems that had already presented themselves, problems which he knew would not be solved until he had taken heavy risks. It was quite clear that his original orders had not taken into account even a small percentage of the actual troubles involved in the case.

His store clothes went into the carpetbag and he dressed himself in the range garb which he had worn for his night scout. This morning, however, he substituted well-worn Texas boots for the lighter footgear of the previous evening. Then, after a moment's hesitation, he buckled a gun belt around his lean hips. If Marshal Ross Doyle wanted to wake up early and fuss with an outgoing traveler about a violation of his pet gun ordinance, McCall was in just the proper mood to have it out with him. He was getting pretty well primed for a mild experiment with the giant lawman. Nothing to give the hand away, of course; just a probing job which might tip him off to the big man's real character.

Doyle was not on the streets, however. For that matter no one was. McCall did not see a single person as he covered the short distance from the Silver Strike to Langan's Lone Star Livery. The easy, comfortable silence of early morning hung over the railroad sidings, the new steel water tank and the half dozen dreary little buildings north of the rail line. A red sun, just coming into view above the eastern mountains, seemed like a giant headlight approaching along the gleaming rails which split the pass. It brightened the escarpments of the Wapitis to the north and softened the shadows of the green slopes to the south and west. It even made the town look less bleak, which was a major accomplishment, even for the sun.

McCall grinned a little more cheerfully as he saw the stable's big sign gleaming in that sunlight. Shorty Langan had lived in New Mexico territory for thirty years but he still insisted on being a staunch Tejano. It was a part of the man's character, just as was his eternal pessimism. Shorty was never very cheerful about anything, but he was dependable. That was enough for McCall.

He saw quickly enough that the liveryman had been true to his promise. There was a tough, rangy chestnut in the stable yard, already saddled and with the usual equipment of the range rider. From the open door of Langan's living quarters came an appetizing odor of bacon, flapjacks and coffee. McCall decided that maybe the morning wasn't going to be so bad after all.

In spite of his confidence in Langan he had made up his mind to keep his own counsel. Shorty was honest enough but he was not always discreet. He might let something slip and it didn't pay to take chances on a chore like this one. Consequently, McCall simply related his evening's adventures up to the point where he had gone to the hotel to change clothes.

Langan twisted his narrow features until a few additional wrinkles crowded into the already seamy countenance. "It sounds right ornery to me, Larry," he said worriedly. "It don't seem like anybody would be gettin' after ye just fer nothin'. Got any idea what they might be after?"

"I figured you might be able to make a guess. The man they jugged was named Jake Zellers."

Langan started in surprise. "That's funny. Jake ain't much of a feller but I never figgered him fer a back-alley road agent. But then ye can't always tell a book by the company it keeps, as the poet says."

McCall laughed aloud. "Now I feel right at home. I've heard one of the famous Langan perverted proverbs."

The little man grimaced. "Don't git smart. I know what I mean."

"It's a good thing somebody does. What about this Jake Zellers? What's his line of business?"

"He ain't got one. Always seems to have enough to live on, though. I wonder if . . . ?"

"You wonder what?" McCall prompted as the stableman's voice dwindled away.

"I don't rightly know. Sometimes I ain't certain I oughta trust Ross Doyle. He puts on a plumb smart show o' makin' Latigo a respectable village but some queer things happen around here. Nothin' a man could put a finger on but jest little things that add up to a right suspicious smell. Like the old sayin' goes, when there's a heap o' smoke it stands to reason somebody musta struck a match."

"But you don't have any idea what's going on?"

"Nope. And I ain't been tryin' too hard to find out. There's enough trouble in this here cockeyed vale o' tears without a man rushin' around to find more. Sufficient unto the day is the gol-derned cussedness thereof, I always say."

McCall chuckled. "Sound wisdom if not a very good quotation," he commented. "Do I smell breakfast?"

"Ye sure do. I said I'd have it ready, didn't I?"

33

"Then lead me to it. I'd like to get out of this place before something else decides to happen."

The talk ran to lighter topics, mostly harking back to the old days, and McCall made short work of the substantial meal Langan had provided. Then he paid his bill and prepared to ride. He was not expecting any further trouble in Latigo but he was alert as he stepped out into the sunshine. There was always the chance that the enemy might have switched tactics. Last night the talk had indicated an unwillingness for further violence in Latigo but plans could change. McCall was in no position to take chances.

The consciousness of danger was strong enough to over-ride Shorty Langan's continuing chatter, strong enough to make McCall look around quickly as he moved out into the open. That was how he happened to get a glimpse of the man who was ducking out of sight behind an adjacent building. McCall could not be certain but the lurking form had seemed oddly familiar. He would have offered odds that Jake Zellers was out of jail and on scout duty again.

Suddenly he wondered whether this was simply a scouting job. Maybe there had been a change of plan at the enemy's headquarters. In that case Zellers might have been sent out to do a bit of dry-gulching. McCall pulled up short, turning his head to shoot a quick warning at Shorty Langan. Just as he did so, however, the shuffle of a footstep came to him from directly in his rear.

He whirled instantly to spring away from the stable door which Langan was partially blocking. With the body movement his right hand swept down and across, bringing up a forty-five in a gesture which was too quick for the eye to follow. It left him in a tense crouch, his gun leveled at the lanky, unshaven man who had just come around the corner of the stable.

There was a grunt of surprise from the stranger,

echoed by an admiring chuckle from Shorty Langan. Then McCall flushed and rammed the gun back into leather. The stranger was obviously unarmed.

"Gettin' nervy, I reckon," McCall acknowledged with a wry smile. "Sorry, partner."

The lanky man grinned, showing white teeth which gleamed unexpectedly out of the bewhiskered, sunburned countenance. He was a rough looking specimen except for the teeth and the pair of clear blue eyes which studied McCall amusedly. "Mighty sudden draw, mister," he drawled. "I'm right glad I wasn't the ranny yo' was expectin' to see."

McCall was still a little red. "I'll have to be careful with that performance. It was great stuff to show folks from the stage, but out here it'll look like a guilty conscience actin' up."

"I reckon I understand," the lanky one commented. "Likewise I'm beginnin' to see how come Jake Zellers got played for a fool last night."

Something about him struck a chord of memory then and McCall knew that this was the man he had heard referred to as Wells. The man who was new to the Doyle gang, probably new to Latigo Pass. "You needn't mention it to the marshal," he said easily, trying to cover his quick suspicion. "No need for him to get burned about me carrying a gun in town; I'm on my way out."

"It's yore business," the lanky man said, and turned away.

Shorty Langan chuckled again. "Was that fast draw part of yer show, Larry?"

"Sure."

"I figured it musta been. Ye didn't used to be any kind of a gun hand as I recall, and that job looked like plenty o' practice to me. Purty good joke when ye think about it; a shore enough westerner goes east to learn gun slingin'."

"Did you know that fellow?" McCall asked, brushing aside the pleasantries.

"Sure. Name's Wells but I don't know nothin' else about him."

"No matter. He didn't mean anything, I guess. I was just jumpy." He didn't think it worth while to mention his glimpse of Jake Zellers.

"Don't blame ye," Langan sympathized. "After last night ye got a right to expect trouble. Like I always say, expect the worst and if it don't happen ye don't have so much to bellyache about."

McCall laughed. "Now there's a saying that must be all yours, Shorty. If there ever was a cheerful soul who went around expecting the worst it's you."

Langan grinned. "And some day I'll find it, I bet ye. Every silver linin's got a dat-ratted black cloud in front of it, ye know."

McCall swung into the saddle, scanning the immediate neighborhood before starting out of the stable yard. With Jake Zellers lurking in the vicinity he still had to figure on the possibility of trouble.

"Luck," Shorty said. "The bronc is named Albert Sidney Johnston. I most generally call him Sid."

McCall's lips twisted into a smile although his eyes did not lose their alertness. He was quite familiar with the little Texan's habit of naming his broncs after Confederate generals. "Sid's enough," he agreed. "I just hope he's not as unlucky as his famous namesake."

He urged the chestnut out of the yard, deliberately skirting the building which had served as a screen for Zellers Nothing happened and by the time he had circled the adobe he was clear of town, the ragged Wapitis looming in the brightening morning sun ahead of him.

Something like a sigh came to his lips. Latigo Pass and its persistent ill humor was behind. That was a relief, even though he knew that somewhere ahead there would be a ticklish situation involving the man Doyle had sent out on the trail blotting chore. Time enough to think about that part when he faced it; for the moment he knew only a sense of freedom in being out of the town.

It was getting along toward noon when he halted to look back down across the shimmering flats. From that height Latigo Pass looked like a distorted cluster of gray match boxes huddled against twin silver threads, the whole vista twisting and wrinkling in the heat haze. Far to the south the mountains were green again but the pass itself was the dingy tan of the alkali. Even from a distance Latigo Pass was not a pretty town.

He grimaced as he traced the winding trail which he had ascended. It made its laborious, twisting way among the rocks and mesquite clumps which studded the face of the mountain barrier, finally leveling off here where a narrow gulch offered entrance into the heart of the Wapitis. Far to the west a plume of mixed black and white heralded the approach of an eastbound train but it was a tiny dark speck at the edge of the alkali which had brought the frown to McCall's sweaty features.

He studied the figure carefully for several minutes but reached no useful conclusion. The distance was too great for recognition and he could only suppose that the Latigo crowd had sent another man into the Wapitis. Someone to check on Olson, perhaps.

That Olson, or some other agent, had been sent ahead was a matter of no possible doubt. Many times during the climb McCall had seen the sign of an earlier rider on the trail and some of that sign had been peculiarly informative. Twice on the lower slopes the man had evidently wandered from the trail, but after that he had stuck closely to the increasingly difficult path. To Mc-Call's mind that spelled a quick answer. The other rider had started the climb during the hours of darkness, just as Doyle had been instructed. He had lost the trail a couple of times but had done better on the higher slopes because daylight had come to aid him.

McCall grinned happily at his own thoughts. Maybe he hadn't lost his touch at his business. Those years in the east had not caused him to lose the knack of reading sign for all it was worth. Too bad he didn't have something more cheerful to read.

He turned then and rode into the steep walled gulch which marked the end of the main climb. This was the real entrance into the Wapiti badlands and the trail would be easy to ride but hard to read from this point on. Olson, if that was the earlier rider's name, would have left precious little sign on the rocks which floored most of the canyon ahead.

Within a quarter mile the gulch became a canyon and McCall watched his prediction come true. It was almost impossible to find any trace of Olson's passage. Still he knew that he could not afford to miss anything of importance. He had to learn something of the other man's errand.

It was equally certain that he did not dare to be openly curious or suspicious. Those orders to Doyle had been clear. Olson was to go into hiding after his trail blotting efforts, watching to see whether McCall would show any signs of knowing too much. He was to keep shady except in an emergency, but McCall knew well enough that any show of curiosity would constitute that emergency. He could only hope that Olson was not given to much imagination. It was not a comfortable feeling to know that life depended upon the emotional stability of an unknown outlaw.

He remembered the canyon passage well enough as he let the chestnut idle through it. This had been the regular trail to Latigo Pass in the days when he had been chore man for Pop at K-Bar. The Latigo trail, they had called it then. Here it was a narrow, steep walled gorge but a half mile ahead there would be a confused jumble of broken rocks where several canyons and gulches came together. The Latigo trail led straight through and into another rocky passage which led down into the pleasant valley of the K-Bar. To the best of his memory there were no other important breaks in the canyon walls so he fully expected that the intersection would be the spot of strategic interest, the spot where he had to learn something without showing it.

He knew that Olson was deliberately keeping to the bare rock now, going out of his way to avoid leaving sign. That made it seem certain that the critical point was not far ahead. It brought a feeling of tension which he could not quite overcome but he fought it down, making himself lounge a little in the saddle as the chestnut broke out into a tangle of split rocks, mesquite thickets, grassy patches and scattered pines. This was the strange little valley which served as the focal point for several badlands passages and suddenly McCall remembered the name he had heard mentioned in that conversation at the jail. Devil's Cockpit! That described it exactly. Now he knew that he had to put on a good act. Somewhere nearby a man named Olson was probably watching him over gunsights.

He pulled up easily, looking around him with what he hoped was an air of casual interest. He knew that he had to appear as a tired rider permitting his horse a breather, but he managed to get a pretty good look at the ground around him while he was making the necessary motions. There were no tracks visible.

He had never paid much attention to this freakish valley in the old days but now he saw that it was simply a shallow depression among the Wapiti crags. Those low, pine-clad hills to the west were really the tops of high mountains while behind the escarpment to the north were the crags which blocked off Latigo Pass from the gentler valley in which K-Bar herds ought to be fattening. Only to the east was the country unknown to him. He had never found time to explore in that direction.

He threaded his way among the rocks, swinging to the right and studying the yawning entrance to a canyon which led into the unknown east. There were no footprints anywhere near the opening, the loose dirt being as smooth as though the rains and winds had been grooming it for an eternity. Then his quick eye caught a hint of what he had been expecting to find. On the bare rock of the canyon's entrance there were numerous scratches and nicks.

He did not pause but rode slowly on to where a second cut appeared in the rock wall. This was the trail to K-Bar and he knew that he would have to take it without further delay. One move into the wrong canyon and there would be an end to the investigations of Larry McCall.

He chuckled grimly as he let the chestnut pick up a faster pace. Olson had done a remarkably good job of trail blotting back there in the Devil's Cockpit. He had gotten rid of sign indicating the passage of riders across the opening, but he had not been able to do anything about those telltale marks on the bare rock. The scrape and dig of iron-shod hooves could not be erased so easily. A lot of traffic must have gone through into that eastern canyon.

It was no surprise to find the trail innocent of sign now. Olson's job had ended back there at the intersection. McCall tried again to remember something about that other canyon but his memory would not come up with a thing. It must have been one of the few badland trails which he had never explored. So far as he knew the passage could lead almost anywhere—and be used for almost any purpose.

Another hour found him still in the crag country but the trail was leading gradually down grade now, the canyon walls sloping away in places until the rugged character of the country was almost lost. Presently he broke away from rock walls entirely and found himself on a wooded bench which overlooked a green valley many times as large as the one back there in the crags. The ground dropped away to the north and west, sloping to where a stream sparkled among the trees. Beyond the stream on the west was another rocky plateau but to the north the country was open, billowing out into open range where green rolling hills made a marked contrast to the grays and browns of the badlands. Below him and a little to the right were buildings and corrals. This was the place Larry McCall had once called home.

As he worked his way down the wooded slope he knew that many changes had been made in the little cluster of buildings which marked K-Bar's headquarters. Additional corrals had been constructed, the ranch house had been altered and repaired, a water system of some sort with windmill power had been installed near the creek, and the lower meadow was securely fenced. It did not look like the rundown establishment he had expected to find. Surely this was not the work of the incapable sort of person Tanner was reported to be.

No one stirred around the house and McCall rode in slowly, studying the place with an eagerness that was vaguely disturbing. After all, his errand here was a casual one, almost a blind for his real errand. He did not have any right to feel this way but he knew that such was the case. Maybe he had been expressing his true thoughts when he gave Shorty Langan that nice lecture on the joys of being a ranchman.

He turned the chestnut into the empty corral and strode toward the low log house with its well-tended dooryard and brightly colored curtains. That was another surprise. Jim Tanner's wife had been dead for over a year, Langan had said, and the old man's daughter was just a gangling kid in her teens. But somebody had been doing a first rate job of homemaking.

The thought was in his mind when a feminine voice sounded sharply from somewhere in the cabin. "Stop right there, mister! I've got a rifle aimed at you and I'll shoot if you come another step!"

5

McCall halted. There didn't seem to be any choice in the matter. A suspicious movement behind one of the flowered curtains indicated the position of the speaker while the tone of the words hinted at determination rather than nervousness. Either Jim Tanner had found himself a staunch new wife or that spindly daughter had grown up into something mighty pert.

"No need to get excited," McCall soothed. "I didn't come to rob the place or burn it down. Is Mr. Tanner around?"

"Of course he is!"

McCall chuckled silently. For the first time there was a hint of nerves in the obvious falsehood. A woman who fears to be found alone is always ready to announce the menfolks as being close at hand. "Call him for me, will you? He'll know me."

"What's your business?"

"Private. Are you Mrs. Tanner?"

"No."

"Well, that's neither here nor there. It's none of my business what women are around the place."

"Don't talk like an idiot! Jim Tanner is my father!"

"Good. Maybe we can understand each other. Certainly we have met before. I'm Larry McCall. Remember me?"

The curtain twitched just a little as though a gun muzzle had brushed it. Suddenly McCall realized how

42

thoughtless he had been. Certainly Jim Tanner's daughter would have grown up. Five years had passed.

The girl seemed to be studying him. Her voice was a little less stern as she said, "Maybe you're McCall. I don't know for sure. Tell me something about yourself so I'll be certain."

"Want a password, eh? All right. I left here because I got an itch to see the world. I made a deal with Jim Tanner to run the place on shares—and I've never collected any shares. Does that mean anything to you?"

The curtain moved again and he had a feeling that she had not liked his bluntness. Her voice was cold when she finally agreed, "I guess you're McCall. Come on in."

He was a little surprised when she met him at the door. After the short conference he had expected to see a pretty tough-looking female, but this girl did not suggest guns and threats; she reminded him of the neat curtains and the well-kept yard. Even the Winchester in her hand could not detract from the charm of her pleasantly oval face and the soft brown hair. A neatly cut gingham housedress set off the slim lines of her figure even as it advertised her neatness. Jim Tanner's gangling daughter had turned into quite a pretty young woman.

"Sorry I sounded so gruff," she said, her eyes troubled even as she tried to smile. "My father is on the lower range this afternoon and I didn't want to take chances with a stranger coming from your direction."

McCall did not miss the point but he elected to ignore it for the time being. Soon enough to inquire about the Latigo trail when he understood the K-Bar situation a little better. Maybe by that time some of the hostility would go out of those wary brown eyes that were watching him so intently.

"Your father will be back this evening?" he asked.

"Any time now. Won't you come in?" She was being gracious even though she could not quite conceal her displeasure. He thought he could understand that part;

the daughter of a man who was behind in his payments would not be very cordial to a landlord who was in a position to make trouble.

She led the way into a plainly furnished room which still managed to achieve a homey atmosphere. McCall remembered the room well enough, but it had changed remarkably since he had last seen it. Putting the Winchester in a rack she motioned for him to take a large rush-bottomed chair. "Make yourself comfortable," she invited. "Father may be early or he may be late. I never know what to expect."

"Thanks. It's good to get in out of that broiling sun. Want to talk a bit? I'm mighty curious about what you folks have been doing."

"Because you haven't been paid anything, I suppose." The statement was blunt but not particularly sharp.

"It's partly that. But mostly I'm interested in K-Bar and what has been happening to it."

"What do you mean by that?" Even when she frowned there was something pleasant about her smoothly tanned features.

He crossed his legs comfortably and smiled at her, trying to relieve the tension a little. "Maybe I ought to explain a bit," he suggested. "Then you can tell me a thing or two. Fair enough?"

"It depends on what you want me to tell you."

He shrugged it off. There was no discounting her continuing hostility but he did not propose to quarrel with her on that account. "I'll take the chance. When I decided to shuck out of here I was plumb locoed, I reckon. All I knew was that I wanted to get away. I ran across your father in Latigo Pass and made him the proposition to come in on shares. It seemed at the time like an easy way out and a quick one. It would save me the fuss of selling the place and the stock, which was the only thing I thought of then. I didn't know a thing about your father except that he'd come into the territory as a pros-

44

pector but had brought his family along, something prospectors just don't do. I figured a family man might make a go of K-Bar."

The girl nodded quietly. "Father was down and out when he met you. His hopes of quick wealth had gone down the drain but he didn't have anywhere else to go so he stayed here in the territory. My mother and I were pretty happy about it when we found that we would have a decent roof over our heads. Too bad the good luck didn't hold out."

"What went wrong?"

"Everything."

She did not seem inclined to explain so McCall forced the talk with a purposely suggestive comment. "I heard talk in Latigo Pass. People seemed to go out of their way to tell me I needn't expect to get anything out of K-Bar. The general idea was that your father is a poor businessman. They had me expecting to find the place in ruins so I was a little surprised to see the signs of prosperity around."

"Which means that you're suspicious," she flared. "You think my father has been cheating you."

"What would you think if you were in my place?"

"I wouldn't jump at conclusions because idle people let their tongues run!"

"Nor did I. Information is all I want right now."

She quieted down a little, speaking in less angry tones but with the tension still apparent. "We were doing very well at first. Our stock increased, and we sold enough beef to show a profit. At that point my father could have sent you money but he decided to put the profits back into the ranch, buying up some good Brahman stock in an effort to improve the K-Bar herds."

"Fair enough," McCall interrupted. "Profits don't have to show in dollars. Increased values may be more important in the long run."

"But it didn't work out that way in the long run. We

spent money on repairs and we put in the water system. After that we felt we could show a real profit. Then luck turned. My mother died during the winter, and in the spring we began to lose beef. There was never any sign of rustlers on our range but the herd dwindled. Within a year we were in bad straits."

There it was again, the definite hint that an organized rustling outfit operated in this vicinity. In a way it all seemed to hang together, the joke about cheap beef in Latigo Pass, the marks of heavy traffic at the Devil's Cockpit, Ross Doyle's uneasiness at having a stranger riding into the Wapitis. The only flaw seemed to be the lack of sign along this end of the Latigo trail. McCall would have sworn that no cattle had gone through that passage in weeks.

"How long ago did you suffer your most recent loss?" he asked suddenly.

"Almost three months. We haven't been troubled since we hired the new hand."

McCall frowned. "You make it sound as though there were a connection. Do you figure that the new man's good enough to scare rustlers away?"

"Maybe there's no connection at all. I just mentioned the fact. There was a fellow named Surrat riding for us but he complained all the time, mostly because he did all the errands in Latigo Pass and was afraid to make the trip. Twice he claimed that somebody took pot shots at him but we thought he was just talking. Finally he left. Next day this man Glennister turned up, asking for the job. He said he'd come out from Mesa."

"Mesa? That's the town about thirty miles north of here, isn't it?"

"That's right. Anyway, Walt Glennister persuaded my father that we should make Mesa our trading and shopping center, keeping clear of Latigo Pass. Since then we have lost no stock." She made a wry face as she added, "Not that we have so very much to lose."

46

"Sounds like a right odd coincidence—if it is one."

She made no reply. McCall covered the awkward pause by building a smoke, first getting her nod of consent. He wanted time to think and it was a little difficult to keep his mind on rustlers while Miss Tanner was sitting there in front of him.

Finally she broke in with a blunt question. "Did you come back here to take the place over?"

He met her eyes squarely. "I'm thinking along those lines. A good ranch is the place for a man once he gets done having crazy ideas about excitement."

She stood up quickly, her lips tight. "Then you do intend to step in and take over the results of my father's efforts!"

"I didn't say so."

"You might as well!" Before he could say another word she almost ran from the room, a suspicion of a sob floating back to him as she disappeared.

McCall grimaced and climbed to his feet, hesitating uncertainly before moving out into the afternoon sunshine once more. Evidently his visit to K-Bar was not going to be any more of a picnic than had been his evening in Latigo Pass. Which was a shame, too. With a girl like Miss Tanner around the place a fellow might hope for something better.

For the rest of the afternoon he loafed restlessly around the ranch house, looking over the ingenious water system by which the house and stable were supplied from the clear mountain creek and studying the various other improvements Tanner had made or started. It was easy to see why his arrival at K-Bar had been met with resentment and suspicion. The place had the makings of a mighty fine spread, thanks to the efforts of the Tanners, but the run of bad luck had left them pretty much at the mercy of the returning landlord. McCall knew that he was in a position to claim everything in sight and he understood why the girl would look at

47

him with suspicion. He even felt a little guilty although he had no intention of injuring the Tanners.

In a somewhat less personal fashion he felt guilty about letting himself get so interested in K-Bar and its rustling troubles. The ride out here had been made primarily as a blind and secondarily because his treatment in Latigo Pass had made him curious. His real business in this country would be down there around the silver mines, and he knew that he ought to be handling that problem before he started probing into this one. It wasn't giving the Apache Company a fair shake to accept their fee and then spend the time running down rustlers. It didn't even make good sense.

The sun had already dropped behind the ragged escarpments west of the creek when McCall spotted two riders approaching from the open country down the creek. As they drew nearer he saw that one was the lean old man who had accepted his proposition that day in Latigo Pass while the other was a big, gangling rider who looked clumsy in the saddle. McCall promised himself that he would keep a sharp eye on this man Glennister. Maybe the fellow was just a smart ranch hand and maybe he was something else. That business of avoiding Latigo Pass sounded like an idea that might have been planted by Doyle's crowd.

The two men came on at a gallop when they spotted him, but cut the pace again as the girl came out to stand by the door. McCall walked across toward her. "Thanks for putting in an appearance. For a minute I was afraid your pappy was going to come a-shootin'. You folks don't trust strangers much, do you?"

"We just mind our own business," she·retorted, refusing to smile at his pleasantry. "At least we'd like to."

The sharpness of the rebuke stung him to a retort of his own. "Mindin' business is a mighty fine thing," he observed, drawling the words until he reminded himself of Shorty Langan springing one of those pet proverbs of his. "For five years now I haven't been doing it. Now I'd better get started."

She turned away from him without a word and went back into the house.

McCall kept his eyes on the approaching riders, presently noting Jim Tanner's start of recognition. The old man seemed to bend his lean body forward in the saddle as though squinting hard, then he spoke swiftly to his companion. By that time they were close enough for McCall to read their expressions and he knew that they were not welcoming him with any more cordiality than the girl had displayed.

Still he tried to hide his feelings as the pair dismounted and started toward him. Jim Tanner's face was a study but he swallowed hard and took the hand McCall offered. Glennister held back, making no attempt to conceal his surly distrust.

"I been wonderin' about ye, McCall," Tanner informed him. "I suppose ye're wantin' to know how come ye never got any money outa the place?"

"Your daughter has been telling me about that. But I don't believe I came entirely on that account. I'm interested in the ranch in general."

"Which means ye're figurin' on takin' over, I reckon." Tanner made it a simple statement of fact but he could not hide the bitterness in his voice.

"Don't jump at conclusions," McCall replied, still trying to keep things easy. "I haven't made any hasty decisions since I leased you the place, and I'm not proposing to make any now. We'll talk things over when you're ready."

Tanner nodded, a shade of relief showing in the tired old eyes. "After supper," he agreed. "Walt, take care o' the broncs, will ye? I'll talk to Mr. McCall." He jerked a thumb over his shoulder at the heavy-jawed young man who stood behind him. "Walt Glennister. He's been workin' for me fer a couple o' months now. Walt, this is Larry McCall, owner of K-Bar."

Walt Glennister stared with open hostility at McCall. "Yuh come in from Latigo?" It was an accusation rather than a query.

McCall's suspicions flared anew. There was only one reason why Glennister should be interested in such a matter. "Naturally I did," he said quietly. "Why not? Latigo's the best rail connection."

"Mesa's safer," Glennister grumbled. Then he turned away, leading both broncs toward a small corral which McCall had noted behind the stable.

Tanner seemed to think an explanation necessary. "We stopped usin' Latigo Pass," he said nervously. "Mighty rough crowd over there since the silver mines started runnin' full blast. Too close to the border to be safe, and there was the chance that some of the worst outlaws would use the Wapitis for a hangout. Mesa's farther but it's safer."

"Latigo's still a good market town for a beef outfit," McCall reminded him. "I'd think K-Bar might work up a nice trade there."

"We'll talk about it after supper. I suppose ye met my daughter Helen?"

"Over a gun. She didn't like my looks."

"Ye mean she didn't remember ye?"

"No. But that's not surprising. I didn't remember her, either." Then he added silently, "But I will."

The supper table conversation was not exactly lively. McCall did not want to force the issue by asking too many questions and the others seemed reluctant to express themselves. Jim Tanner fumbled helplessly and Helen made it clear that she did not intend to ease matters for the interloper. Glennister maintained a dour silence but his cold gray eyes were upon McCall constantly. It seemed like a fair guess that the K-Bar rider was wondering about the stranger's journey up from

50

Latigo Pass. He couldn't be sure just how much McCall might have seen in the Devil's Cockpit.

In spite of the tension, however, McCall managed to get a pretty good picture of the situation from Tanner, much the same picture he had already gotten from the girl. K-Bar was actually prospering but Tanner had not been willing or ready to take a profit. He had turned earnings into additional capital, spending money for blooded cattle to improve the K-Bar herd and adding to the real estate. In another year or two, he claimed, they would have had one of the finest spreads in the southwest. But then the rustling troubles had started, a mysterious series of stock thefts which had been completely baffling. The herd had been depleted until now the ranch was in a bad way.

McCall was willing to take him at his word. The old man was not the type to make fancy promotion talk; what he claimed was likely to be true. Moreover, his ideas sounded like good sound business. Certainly the condition of the house and corrals bore out his claims.

"Naturally I'll want to look the place over," McCall told him finally. "If I agree on your course of action I won't interfere. I do think, however, that something should be done to put the law on the trail of the rustlers. And I think it would be well to start making a play for the beef market in Latigo Pass. The town is booming and the mines are using large quantities of meat for the workmen. If we don't want to reduce the herd any further just now we can still sell some culls and get ourselves a connection with a market that may turn out to be mighty profitable later on."

"Better forget Latigo," Walt Glennister growled. "Drivin' steers through that canyon country ain't healthy."

"Any reason to say that?" McCall asked mildly.

"Of course he has!" It was Helen Tanner who had answered the question. "He knows what our conditions are here because he has been on the ground and doing the work."

McCall let a corner of his mouth droop into a quizzical smile. "Meaning that I'm not as well qualified to make a judgment?"

"Take it that way if you wish."

Jim Tanner broke in then. "You keep outa this, Helen," he snapped. "McCall still owns the place, ye know."

"He's not letting us forget it," the girl retorted.

They finished the meal in a rather strained silence, only Jim Tanner making a feeble effort to keep conversation going. It was the old man, too, who tried to break the tension when the meal was over. He set an example by assuming a share in the kitchen chores and McCall hastened to follow suit. For the next quarter hour all four of them worked together but there was no good humor in it.

After they returned to the main room it was no better. Somewhat to McCall's surprise, Walt Glennister sat in on the conference, apparently accepted as an interested party. It seemed like a peculiar way for a hired hand to act, and McCall began to wonder about Glennister's real status in the Tanner home. Maybe he was the real reason why Helen displayed so many neat habits of housekeeping. The way she had sprung to his defense hinted that such might be the case.

The thought made McCall a little abrupt in his comments as Tanner went over his whole story in added detail. The old man was talking a little more hopelessly now, as though convinced that he was about to lose everything. McCall sensed the feeling, but he knew that he could not afford to commit himself yet. He had to understand a number of things, including the Glennister angle, before he could reassure Tanner. Better to let the old man think harshly of him than to spoil everything by talking too much and too soon.

Still it made for an uncomfortable evening and no one offered any objection when McCall proposed to break it up. They displayed a rather uncomplimentary promptness in sending him off to the bunkhouse under convoy of the sullen Glennister. The fact didn't help his frame of mind any, and he knew a quick resentment when Glennister left him alone in the bunkhouse. Evidently there was to be more talk this evening, but not while Larry McCall was around.

6

When McCall rolled out of his blankets at the first peep of dawn he knew that he had slept rather well. A long day of riding coming hard after that rough night in Latigo Pass had left him so weary that even his troubled thoughts had not been able to keep him awake. He dimly remembered hearing Glennister come into the bunkhouse but he had not heard the man get up for work. A glance from the window, however, indicated that both Tanner and his hired man were busily engaged with ranch chores. Whatever else might be said for the Tanner establishment, it was not a lazy one.

The thought helped him to shake off some of the resentment which remained from the previous evening but the mood did not last long. When he joined Tanner, just in time to answer the breakfast call, he discovered that cordiality was to be the keynote of the morning. Tanner made jokes, Glennister went out of his way to be genial, and Helen had suddenly become a most gracious hostess. The change was too abrupt to be anything but suspicious and he found himself wondering what it meant. Evidently they had held a pow-wow late last evening and had decided to give him the sweet treatment. But why? Did it mean that they really had something to hide, or was it simply that Tanner had made the other two see the uselessness of antagonizing a man who could become troublesome? Either way McCall did not like the idea.

"Want to look over the herd today, McCall?" Tanner asked when breakfast was nearly over.

"Maybe this afternoon. I'm kinda feeling the urge to see the country a mite. It makes a man have a lot of memories when he comes back to a place like this after five years. I'll mosey around a bit and keep out of your hair this morning, then we'll get down to brass tacks this afternoon. All right with you?"

"Yuh don't need to hold back none," Walt Glennister· growled, dropping his forced good nature. "There ain't nothin' we ain't willin' for yuh to see right now."

McCall studied him frankly. Glennister must be securely in the confidence of the Tanners—or he had some kind of a hold on them. McCall could only hope that it would not turn out to be the latter. "I'm willing to believe that," he said, keeping his voice unconcerned. "If I didn't think the place was all right, I'd be right with you this morning."

They took that in silence, exchanging only brief glances. McCall followed it promptly, making a bid for confidence. He did not know yet whether he wanted that confidence for strategic purposes or for something more sincere. Either way it couldn't do any harm.

"I know you folks figure I'm going to be a nuisance to you so let's settle a couple of points right now. In the first place I'm not going to make any fuss about lack of profit if I find that you've been doing a smart job of building up K-Bar. In the second place I'm not trying to steal either profit or capital gain away from you. I do, however, have a hunch that I'm going to declare myself back in the cattle business. Chasing around the country may be all right for a young hellion like I was when I left here, but I'm old enough to know better now. This

54

place suits me fine. You can be thinking that over and one of these days we'll talk turkey. I reckon there's enough so nobody will have to get skinned by anybody else." In a way it was the same talk he had given Shorty Langan, but this time he knew that he meant every word of it.

There was a moment of silence and then Helen Tanner said acidly, "Which means that you expect to cut yourself in on the profits my father has been building up."

"Profits he has been building on my capital," McCall reminded her. "After all, you people have had a living out of this place for five years. Do you think you could have done any better elsewhere and still have good prospects ahead?"

The girl flushed, but her father broke in hurriedly. "I reckon ye're bein' fair enough, McCall. We ain't complainin' 'til we've had a chance to talk facts and figgers."

"Suits me," McCall retorted. "I just wanted you to know where I stand."

He took his time after breakfast, staying out of the way while Tanner and Walt Glennister saddled to ride off down the slope into the lower valley. Then he threw his rig on the chestnut and set off in the opposite direction. K-Bar seemed to be in a condition that would keep; the more immediate source of worry was the mystery of that cross canyon back in the crags. The rustler trail, he was beginning to name it in his own mind.

His thoughts were full of a possible connection between rustling and the Latigo Pass matter as he sent the chestnut into the steep ascent at the southwest curve of the valley. The climb was pretty tough here but he knew that it would lead him to a rocky plateau which overlooked the valley itself, a barren mesa which stretched from the Latigo trail canyon to the gorge which carried the creek into the valley. Its southern

55

border, he felt sure, would be that winding succession of gulches and valleys which would have to be the rustlers' pathway.

He paused at the top of the climb, studying the rolling valley below him and tracing the course of Clear Creek from the gorge to the abundant grasslands which Tanner was using for his grazing range. Without question K-Bar had the makings of a mighty fine spread; only a young hairpin with more energy than brains would have left it in the first place.

Almost at once he saw a rider on the distant slope and knew it to be Jim Tanner. Walt Glennister was not in sight and McCall concluded that the rider had worked into the timber, probably rounding up as many head of cattle as possible for the coming inspection. Tanner would be out to make as good a showing as possible.

Then he swung away from the cliff's edge and headed back into the crags at a steady pace which put distance behind him without exhausting his bronc. He smiled a little as he recalled that his father had always called it "Sheridan's pace," claiming that this mile-eating gait had been largely responsible for the general's strategic successes.

"I hope you don't feel hurt, General Albert Sidney Johnston," he said aloud to the pony. "Shorty might object to copying after a Yank but I reckon you won't mind."

Within twenty minutes he struck a landmark that he remembered, a deep canyon which stretched north and south across the rocky plateau as though the whole stony mesa had split itself lengthwise. It was blind on its northern end, not quite reaching to the line of cliffs which flanked the K-Bar valley, but he had never explored it to its southern extremity. He could only guess that it would lead him to that succession of valleys which lay west of the Devil's Cockpit. One way or another it offered a fair path to the south.

He followed the yawning crevice until he found the steep path which he had once used to reach the canyon's floor. There he dismounted, leading the bronc as he worked his way down the treacherous incline to the relatively level floor of the cut. For a mile to the south he knew that the canyon wound its twisted way among the crags, but beyond that point he had never ventured.

He watched for sign as he reached the lower level and climbed back into the saddle but there was nothing to indicate that anyone had been down in this rocky defile since last he had ventured here. Apparently the rustler trail did actually continue into the west. He pushed on easily, trying to keep his sense of direction even as he estimated the distance he was riding. It might turn out that the information would be useful.

Shortly after he passed the limit of his previous explorations the canyon widened and became a little more shallow so that he lost the feeling of being deep in the solid rock of the mesa. It was clear that this gulch roughly paralleled the Latigo trail so he felt sure that it would lead him into those winding valleys which he knew would lie west of the Devil's Cockpit. Somewhere in that region would be the rustlers' trail.

Then the defile petered out entirely, the ravine blocked off by a slope of tumbled rocks which led to the higher ground of the plateau itself. Again McCall dismounted, leading his bronc as he climbed the treacherous slope. Within a matter of three or four minutes he was among the crags again, mounting for a continued push into the south. This time it was a short ride. He had started to build a smoke as he settled himself in the saddle, but before he could strike a light he found himself approaching a deep opening. His hunch told him that this would be the cross valley he had expected to find.

He eased the bronc over a little ledge of solid rock and pulled up to stare down into the depths. The place was

57

rocky but it was not just a split in the solid stone of the mesa; it was a valley rather than a canyon. McCall studied the ground briefly, then sent the chestnut cautiously down the grade to where he had spotted the definite marks of a well-traveled trail. He could not recall the spot exactly, but reason told him that this was a part of the valley he had been thinking about. Certainly it was the trail which led eastward through the Devil's Cockpit.

He dismounted again, studying the welter of hoof marks on the dry ground. Shod and unshod horses had gone through here in either direction while cattle had been driven through from west to east. The westbound sign was obscured in many places but the cattle tracks were comparatively fresh. The whole picture confirmed his belief that the rustling business involved regions to the west of the Wapitis. It also told him that the rustler gang must be somewhere at the eastern end of their circuit. There was nothing here to indicate that they had returned since making their last drive.

He spent a half hour reading signs and trying to make sure of their meaning, following the trail for several hundred yards in both directions. Then he swung back into the saddle and sent the chestnut up the slope over the path by which he had descended. It was a safe bet that this trail was the one Olson had blotted in the Devil's Cockpit, but he knew that it would not be smart tactics to follow it toward that point. A man could find easier methods of committing suicide.

He did not go back into the blind canyon. For a short distance he followed its eastern rim but then he cut away from it, slanting off through the crags toward the Latigo trail. It was hard country on a horse but he took his time, trying to think things out as he rode. It seemed abundantly clear that somebody was using that hidden trail through the Wapitis, somebody who did not want strangers finding it. That was why he had met such peculiar treatment in Latigo Pass. No one had worried about him at first, but they had become seriously concerned when he let it be known that he intended to ride out to K-Bar. They had tried to keep him in town because they were afraid of what he might see in the Devil's Cockpit. When the strong-arm methods failed they had settled for evasion tactics, sending Olson to blot trail. He knew he could thank the Latigo Pass situation for that break. Ross Doyle would have no scruples about methods but he did not want to stir up comment. A large part of the rustler campaign seemed to hinge on the continuing value of Latigo Pass as a blind and a refuge. Which was a good point to keep in mind.

Another fact seemed almost as clear. Doyle and those other rannies in Latigo Pass were not likely to be tangled up in this sort of a deal unless it involved something bigger than a simple bit of cattle stealing. Rustling would not be supporting such a complete organization. Maybe this would turn out to be some kind of key to the mysterious troubles which centered around the silver mines.

The distance across to the Latigo trail was shorter than he had calculated, but he had to search along the familiar cut for some distance before he could find a way to descend into it. It was while he was making the search that he topped a stony ridge and was able to look down a long stretch of straight canyon toward the K-Bar valley. Just rounding a bend to pass out of sight was a rider who looked strangely awkward in the saddle.

McCall pulled up sharply but it was too late to see any more. Glennister was already behind a rocky angle, riding hard toward the ranch.

"Now what?" he said aloud, lips compressed a little grimly. "Let's go, Albert Sidney. We'll have to find out where that polecat has been."

He let the horse circle and work down through a

break that led to the canyon floor but even before he saw the double set of tracks he knew what Glennister's errand had been. The K-Bar rider had hustled down to the Devil's Cockpit to pass the word about McCall's ride into the badlands. That was why he had not been in the lower valley with Tanner earlier in the day.

"Makin' it tough for me, is he?" McCall grimaced. "I might have expected something like this."

He was finding it hard to choke back the anger. This business had been dangerous enough while the Latigo gang accepted him as just a casual intruder. Now the risk would be sharply increased. This would' be the emergency mentioned in Olson's orders, the emergency calling for gunplay. From now on Larry McCall would be fair game for any outlaw gun that could be brought to bear on him—and he could thank Walt Glennister for putting him on that hot spot.

For a moment he considered the chance that Jim Tanner was equally involved with Glennister, but decided that there was no way to make a judgment on that point. All he could hope to do now was to check on Glennister's movements, and perhaps make a play before the rustlers could take concerted action.

In spite of the danger of the situation he was eager as he headed the chestnut toward the Devil's Cockpit. Maybe this would be his chance to have a look at that significant intersection. If Glennister had taken his news to Olson it seemed likely that the watcher would have carried it on, perhaps leaving the rustler trail unguarded. In any event it would be better to scout the place now than to wait until later. The rustlers would soon throw men enough into the little valley so that there would be no chance of Larry McCall getting through to spill the beans about their dirty game.

He rode at a good pace until he knew that he was within a quarter mile of the intersection, then he dismounted and picketed the chestnut in a clump of mesquite which filled one of the canyon's irregular breaks. After that he climbed to the rimrock on the east side and slipped cautiously forward, keeping a wary eye out for any guard who might be posted atop the canyon walls.

There was nothing to be seen but rocky pinnacles, loose boulders and an occasional stunted piñion, but he did not relax his vigilance as he worked toward the rocky tongue which separated the K-Bar trail from that mysterious eastern canyon. This was no time to be inviting bushwhack bullets.

It seemed almost too easy and he had still seen no sign of life when he slid into a position from which he could overlook the entire intersection. Directly below him were the tracks Walt Glennister had left and he studied them first. They swung hard to the left as they left the K-Bar canyon, turning into that unknown trail which led to the east.

There was nothing else to be seen in the Devil's Cockpit so McCall worked his cautious way across to a point from which he could look down into that eastward passage. This time he saw enough to set his mind at work once more. Just inside the canyon's mouth there was sign to indicate that Glennister had halted, delayed for some time, and then turned back. There was a sizeable niche at that point, with plenty of sign to show that a horse had been picketed there. From the niche a trail led upward across the face of the rock, zig-zagging to a point where the telltale evidence was even more conclusive. Burned matches and numerous cigarette butts were on all sides. This must have been the lookout post for the menacing Olson. But where was Olson now?

McCall studied the trail without going down into the gorge, seeing enough to tell him that this was indeed the rustler trail, the same trail he had studied off there to the west. He also knew that the lookout had gone down to confer with Glennister and had then ridden out into the Devil's Cockpit. Glennister's message had sent Olson on his way, probably to Latigo Pass.

It was only a guess but he could not confirm it from the cliff top. Olson's prints disappeared out there in the little valley and McCall knew that he was going to have to make a gamble. He would have to risk himself in the open in order to know what Olson had actually done.

He stood up cautiously, preparing to retrace his steps to the picketed bronc, and in that instant he heard the distant clatter of a running horse.

He dropped flat, watching from the rimrock, and in another half minute spotted a rider coming out of the valley west of the Devil's Cockpit. He did not know the man by sight but he had no doubt as to his identity. This was Olson, almost without question. The lookout had been tipped off regarding McCall's earlier movements and had ridden west to intercept the intruder. The move had been much too late but it seemed likely that he would have seen the sign of McCall's examination of the rustler trail. His haste indicated that he was not at all pleased with what he had found.

McCall loosened his six-gun in its holster as he waited, but Olson swung his black bronc to the south and disappeared into the canyon which opened out upon the long descent to Latigo Pass. Evidently he had reached the point where he needed new orders and he was riding to town to get them.

The sound of the pounding hooves died away as the man rounded the canyon's first bend and then McCall was in motion, hurrying back to his own mount. Inspection of the K-Bar herd was going to be delayed. More immediate concerns required his presence in Latigo Pass. More than a little grimly he told himself that if he did not go to Latigo today he probably would never reach there. Glennister had stirred up a mighty deadly hornet's nest, and Olson seemed intent on keeping it stirred. It would not be many hours until the rustler gang would have new guards on duty here at this intersection, guards with orders to get rid of a man who was threatening to expose their crooked game.

7

The garish reds and yellows of the Wapitis had long since blurred into dull purples when McCall struck the alkali flat at the base of the mountain barrier. He had not hurried his ride down from the canyon country, partly because he realized that his mount was tiring and partly because he did not want to reach Latigo Pass until after dark. The town would be plenty dangerous for him, he knew, but there was just a chance that his prompt arrival would catch the enemy napping. They would not expect him so close on Olson's heels and he might be able to get his chore done before they could decide on their course of action.

It was dark when he approached those first squatty buildings on the north side of the railroad tracks. He did not believe that his descent of the Wapitis could have been seen from town but he walked his horse, putting on a good show of carelessness to cover the alert caution with which he was searching every shadow. If anyone should be watching him he wanted them to see him as the same casual pilgrim who had been in town two evenings before. The pose probably wasn't any good, not if Olson had really seen anything on that western rustler trail, but while there was any hope of delaying action McCall had to make a play for it. He was not yet ready to force a showdown.

No one challenged him, however, and he rode into Langan's stable yard to find the little liveryman grooming a sweating buckskin in the light of a flaring lantern. McCall remembered that Olson had been riding a black pony so he rejected his own quick hunch that this was the lookout's bronc. Still he was interested. Someone had ridden the buckskin hard not too long ago—and hard riders are usually interesting people, especially in a place like Latigo Pass.

"Looks like somebody's been heelin' that broomtail mighty pert, Shorty," he greeted as he slid stiffly from the saddle. Two days of riding put a lot of tender kinks in a man who had been riding plush for a while.

Shorty stared in the gloom, then chuckled as he recognized his caller. "Ye got back in a hurry, didn't ye? Yep. Ears Trondell ain't easy on broncs. Mostly he's in a dangfired hurry. What brung ye back so fast? In trouble already?"

"Looks like it. The Tanners didn't greet me with what you might call fraternal cordiality. Did you say that was Trondell's horse?"

"Yep. Judgin' by what ye told me the other night he's the jasper that tried to slug ye. Mebbe he heard ye was comin' back to Latigo so he rode in to have another whack at ye. So the Tanners didn't kill the fatted heifer for ye, hey?"

"No. Trondell didn't say anything about me, did he?"

"No. Anything goin' wrong?"

"Such as what?"

"Such as a lot o' things. Mebbe it ain't none o' my show—and it looks like ye're keepin' a tight lip on it— but there's been a heap o' talk around this town about queer doin's up there in the Wapitis. I was beginnin' to believe some o' the talk after what happened to ye here in town the other night. Seemed like somebody was tryin' to keep ye outa the mountains, mebbe because they was afeard ye'd see too much. Then again, I seen Johnny Olson hightailin' it into town from the direction of the Wapitis about an hour ago. I kinda put two and two together, ye might say."

McCall tried to make his quick laugh sound unconcerned. "Shorty, every time you put two and two to-gether you make about seven."

"Trondell kin be the other three. He adds up."

"He come from the Wapitis too?"

"Nope. I kinda had an idea he'd been followin' the rail line from somewhere east of town."

McCall laughed again, letting it cover his quick esti-mate of that information. "You ought to put hobbles on that imagination of yours," he scoffed.

The little man wagged his head sombrely. "Mebbe it ain't all imagination, Larry. Where there's so danged much stink there's bound to be somethin' rotten."

"I won't argue the point. Take care of Albert for me, will you. He's done a couple of hard days' work. Then get another bronc ready in case I might take a sudden notion to get out of town again."

"Like that, hey? I thought so. Well, don't talk about it if ye don't want to. As the feller says, a shut mouth don't catch no blowflies."

McCall chuckled dryly and started away only to turn back hurriedly. "Gosh, I almost forgot and wore a gun into your peaceful little hamlet. Take care of the arsenal for me, will you? If I've got to bank on Doyle's peace-loving prejudices for a while I can't afford to spoil the party by toting a gun."

"Jest be careful," Shorty warned.

McCall left the stable yard and strode across the tracks in the darkness, limbering newly stiffened muscles as he watched on all sides. There was a good chance that he had not yet been spotted, but he did not propose to take unnecessary chances. There was one big gamble that he was due to take and the odds were already against him. No point in making them worse.

He had almost reached the Silver Strike when he caught sight of a towering figure coming across the street from the comparative darkness of the opposite sidewalk. McCall had no desire to bump into Marshal

Ross Doyle just yet so he pulled up abruptly and watched from a doorway while the lawman led two companions into a saloon which stood two doors beyond the hotel. Light from the saloon doors gave McCall a good look at the two men and he felt that he could name them pretty accurately. The shaggy blond hair and sweeping straw-colored mustache he had seen back there in the Devil's Cockpit. The other man's face was not so familiar but those big ears were the tip-off. He had seen their silhouette before.

He caught a glimpse of black hair, a close-cropped black mustache and a big nose. Then the trio disappeared and he was left to think about what he had seen. Ears Trondell and Johnny Olson! Both of them newly arrived in town and already in conference with Ross Doyle. The evening was warming up.

It seemed likely that the enemy were going into a huddle which would bring forth some plan of campaign against Larry McCall. Which meant that McCall had to move quickly, boldly, before such a campaign could get into operation. Accordingly he walked calmly into the Silver Strike, winking genially at the staring proprietor.

"Just couldn't stay away from your steaks, mister," he announced confidentially. "A good reputation is the best kind of advertising, you know."

The stout man seemed confused by the benevolent remark, and McCall strode across to the dining-room doorway. As he had hoped, Gordon Stallcup, the mine company's manager, was eating dinner there. McCall noted that the man was just beginning his meal, so he relaxed a little and turned back to the worried looking innkeeper.

"Got a place handy where a man can sluice off some of the alkali?"

The pudgy man nodded and led the way to a back room where a wash basin and pitcher had been provided.

McCall washed up quickly, making certain that no one was watching him. Then he slid swiftly into a dark corner to fumble with the lining of his left boot. From it he removed a small card which he transferred to a shirt pocket with his tobacco and papers. After that he strolled jauntily into the dining room and helped himself to a vacant chair next to the mining man. It was not entirely pleasant to note that one of the diners was the mild-looking fellow called Jones. Still McCall knew that he had to make his play and make it promptly.

"Evening, Mr. Stallcup," he greeted. "My name's McCall. I used to live around here before you boys started turning the desert into quick money. Now I'm back, so we might as well get acquainted." His breezy air seemed to catch the attention of the other six men in the room, which was his intention. He was playing a part for them quite as much as for the glowering Stallcup.

"I'm planning to run a few head of cattle back there in the Wapitis," he went on briskly. "So I'll be around to talk business with you one of these days. Must take a lot of meat to feed all those miners you've got down at the workings."

Stallcup nodded but did not reply. McCall scarcely gave him an opportunity. "I reckon I know a friend of yours, Mr. Stallcup. Gent by the name of Shaner. I met him when I was tourin' with a show back east. He liked it right well, I reckon. Came around afterwards and talked mighty polite to us. I even got his card somewhere."

He ignored the frown which was making Stallcup's dark face rather forbidding. The mine manager was not a very handsome man, and he was obviously not pleased by this bumptious stranger. The combination made his features quite harsh but there was a questioning glint in his dark eyes as he murmured, "Of course I know Shaner."

67

McCall met the glance significantly but kept up his air of loose-tongued good humor as he produced the card which he had carried in his boot. He made a big show of separating it from cigarette papers before placing it briefly in front of Stallcup's narrowed eyes. "I keep it for a souvenir, you might say. Never had many rich gents like Shaner make so much fuss over my act. Reckon we'll have to get together sometime and swap lies, eh?"

He saw that the ruse had been successful. Stallcup was not accepting this advance with anything like cordiality but he understood—and he was playing up to the occasion. "We'll do that some day," he said, a little stiffly. "How is Shaner, anyway? He's in our company, you know."

"Kind of a big boss, ain't he?"

"Kind of. We do the work out here while he stays back east and collects the profits. That makes him a big boss, I suppose."

McCall laughed loudly and Stallcup used the noise as a cover for a whispered, "Half hour. My office. Know where it is?"

"That's always the way us westerners get skinned," McCall said loudly. "We sure enough will have to have a confab some day. That's your office down the street across from the undertaker's factory, ain't it?"

"That's the place. I'm there most of the time."

They kept it up in that vein until Stallcup left the table. By that time Jones and two of the other diners had left while the others gave no sign that they were interested or had caught any hint of the hidden under-standing between McCall and Stallcup. It was the departure of Jones which reminded McCall that there was a need for haste. Not that the mild-looking little man had been needed to carry word to Marshal Doyle; it was likely that the stout hotelman had done that chore some minutes ago. From now on it would be tough—

68

even if Doyle still persisted in trying to keep the town free from violence.

The street in front of the hotel was becoming pretty noisy by the time McCall left the dining room and suddenly he realized that this was Saturday night. Men would be in from the mines tonight and the town would be in pretty much of an uproar. The fact was worth noting although he couldn't make up his mind that it would help him any. It might keep Doyle occupied with lawman's duties, but it could also mask the sort of violence which otherwise might not be risked.

He had almost forgotten the enigmatic Daisy. She had not appeared as a waitress but he had scarcely noted her absence, being so busy with his act. Now, however, she was at the hotel desk, dressed in the same sort of simple but effective costume as on the earlier occasion. He could not be sure, but he had a hunch that she was waiting to talk with him.

On sudden impulse he decided to follow up the conversation where it had been dropped before, the time when she had offered that cryptic warning.

"Howdy, Daisy," he said, dropping an elbow lazily on the rude desk. "I tried the Wapiti country and lived to tell the tale. What's your gloomy hunch tonight?"

She studied him frankly, trouble blending with curiosity in her dark eyes. "Mister," she said slowly, "either you're a mighty smart hombre or you're awful dumb—and awful lucky."

"Do I get a choice?" Then he saw the irritation in her expression and he added, "Forget I said that. You tried to do me a good turn the other night—and I guess you're hinting at something helpful now. Thanks. I'm not as ungrateful as I may sound."

"Then you'd better put on a pretty good show of telling me a lot of silly things. Act like you're interested in me."

"A plumb easy chore," he told her. "Maybe I am."

69

"Don't try to feed me any of that. But you'll do well to take some more advice." She was smiling again now but he knew that the smile was a part of the pose which she had advised him to try. Obviously they were being watched. She knew it and was warning him of it.

"What kind of advice?"

"Don't go wandering around Latigo Pass tonight."

"Are you giving reasons with the advice?"

"If you're as smart as I'm beginning to think you are, you don't need to be told. If you're as dumb as you pretend to be there's no point in an explanation. Just take my word for it. The streets will be full of drunken miners—Mexicans, Chinese and white riff-raff. It wouldn't take much to start a riot tonight, and innocent bystanders get shot in riots."

"So it's all planned already, is it?"

"I'm guessing. But I think I know the crowd. And don't look so grim. You're supposed to be giving me the usual kind of fast talk, you know."

He relaxed again. "You're a keen hand," he told her. "And I don't want to put you on the wrong side by letting anybody think you're telling me this. Incidentally, you don't want to take the next step and tell me who's after my scalp and why, do you?"

"Maybe I don't know enough to tell," she countered. "I think I've said all I dare say."

"Thanks again. I reckon I know enough."

"Then you must know I'm giving you good advice when I tell you to keep out of the streets."

"I do know it. Better than you gave me last night."

She flushed a little. "Even that was good."

"I mean the first time—when you tried to keep me in Latigo without making it a warning."

"We'd better not talk about that either."

McCall thought swiftly. He knew that he had to get out for his conference with Stallcup but it was clear now that he could not make the trip openly. Neither could he put the girl in a bad spot by using her for his blind.

"You've got a back stairway in this place, haven't you?" he asked finally.

"Yes. It opens into the back yard next to the kitchen door."

"Good. Now pretend you're booking me for a room. Make it a real booking; they'll probably check. Then take me upstairs, preferably to a front room so a guard in the street will see when you light a lamp there. Then you show me the back stairs and trot yourself right back here. Understand?"

"You're still taking a risk. I'm betting there's a guard posted in the back yard."

"I'll be careful. All I'm concerned about now is keeping them from having any idea that you're giving me this help."

Her glance conveyed something which he found a little hard to interpret. Her move, however, was all business. She swung the battered daybook and waited while he made a ritual of writing his name in it. Then she did the honors, escorting him to the upper floor as though he were a newly arrived roomer.

The rest of it went just as he had directed. Daisy lighted a bracket lamp in a front room and McCall showed himself for a brief instant as he drew the shade. Then they went back into the hall and the girl indicated the back stairway. "Do be careful," she whispered.

"I'll try. And thanks again." He waited until she had returned to the lower floor, then he eased himself down the back stairs, cursing the fact that he had to go out unarmed into a roistering town that was full of enemies. Tonight would be the very best time for Doyle and his gang to strike; a killing in Latigo any other night in the week might arouse suspicion, but on Saturday night it would be just an incident to be shrugged off.

He listened at the back door for a full minute before

he even tried the latch. Kitchen noises came clearly enough through the flimsy partition and he could smell stale grease and soapsuds with remarkable clarity. There was no indication, though, of any presence in the back yard.

Finally he opened the door a crack, almost holding his breath for fear of a betraying creak. It seemed like hours before he could look out into the gloom of the night and see an untidy back yard that was partially illuminated by the yellow light from the kitchen windows. There was sufficient illumination for him to spot a watcher immediately, a man who lounged in a shadow at the corner of some sort of outbuilding. The guard was perhaps twenty feet away, so placed that he could see the entire rear of the building. McCall knew that it would be impossible for him to leave without being seen.

He had almost made up his mind to search for a better exit when there was a soft pad of footsteps along the side of the hotel and a thin voice asked, "Are you here, Señor Jake?"

At any other time McCall would have been amused by the grave formality in the faintly accented tones. Now he was only interested in the tall Mexican who had spoken. He could see the fellow clearly enough to know that this was a new character on stage. The tall, conical hat and the elaborately wrapped serape made the man look even taller in the semi-darkness but after the first glance McCall was interested only in the hushed conversation.

"Nacherly," the guard replied, his whisper too much of a grunt to be very secretive. "What's up?"

"Notheeng yet. I am to tell you the man has gone to the upstairs. Señor Doyle theenks he may be remaining for the night." Again there was a marked trace of education in the accent of the Mexican.

"What's Doyle plannin' to do?"

"He ees not decided. Always he fears to make trouble in your fine town."

"Him and his dam' gun laws! Mebbe we can snatch the redhead without makin' no fuss. Tell Ross about the idea."

"You mean to use thees back door to capture your man?"

"That's the idea. No use dependin' on Fatty Knowles if we don't have to. He's scared green already so we'll be better off if we make our play without lettin' him know."

"I tell Doyle," the Mexican agreed. "It ees better if you make sure the door ees not locked." He disappeared into the side alley again and the guard started across toward the partially open door where McCall was waiting. This was the break, McCall knew; he had to make good on this chance or he might never get another one.

8

The guard's identity became clear as soon as he started to pick his way across the untidy yard. It was Jake Zellers and there was plenty of light from the kitchen windows to show that he was wearing a gun. Apparently Zellers was not only immune from serious arrest but he also had the privilege of ignoring Marshal Ross Doyle's anti-gun ordinance. Which was not surprising. There would be more than one armed thug in town tonight, ready to act at the marshal's orders.

Zellers took his time, trying to avoid loose tin cans and at the same time keep out of the lamplight, but finally he slid toward the door, groping a little as though the kitchen lights had thrown his eyes out of focus for darkness. McCall took full advantage of the opportunity. He swung the door wide with his left hand, and put all his weight into the vicious swing which he aimed with his right at Zellers' jaw. Just as had happened on that previous occasion, Zellers went down like a log.

"Glass jaw," McCall muttered grimly as he dropped on the fallen man. "This is getting a little monotonous. I'm always slugging Jake and taking his gun away from him—and where does it get me?" He did not let his own whimsy deceive him, however. This show hadn't even opened yet and even the blundering Zellers might turn out to be a deadly opponent before the final curtain could be rung down.

He paused only long enough to gag the man against an outcry, then he picked him up bodily and carried him away from the hotel, finally dumping him in the shadow of a rickety stable which stood far back in the darkness. Then he did a thorough job of making Zellers helpless. Jake regained consciousness while McCall was lashing his feet together but he was unable to do more than grunt angrily.

"Sorry, Jake," McCall told him. "Too bad to pick on you all the time. Maybe I'll strike bigger game before I'm done."

He rolled the man under a corner of the stable, pausing long enough to slip a few cartridges from the gun belt into his pockets. Then he slid Jake's gun into his shirt front and moved away in the night, following an open strip which he supposed was some sort of back lane.

From the street the noises of Saturday night seemed to be rising a little, either a natural development or a carefully calculated bit of Doyle strategy. A good loud stir in town would be fine cover for whatever plan the crooked marshal had in mind.

Twice he worked in toward the street, trying to get his bearings, and the second time he found himself within a stone's throw of the Apache Mining Company's office. The building was dark, but McCall knew that he could not afford to take chances. Maybe Doyle's spy had been fooled by the casual talk at supper, and maybe not. The place would have to be scouted carefully before he could risk a visit.

It took a quarter of an hour to do the job and by that time he was beginning to fear that Stallcup would not wait for him. The mine manager had not been too cordial, even though he had played up to McCall's lead. It wouldn't do to expect too much of him.

He picked a moment when the street was pretty clear and then went boldly to the front door of the dark office. The door swung open before his quick pressure and Stallcup's voice whispered, "Get in fast. If your business is what I think it is we'll want to talk in the dark."

"Smart idea," McCall approved. "We're poorer targets that way."

"Do you think anyone spotted the game back there at the hotel?"

"Looks like they didn't. I couldn't find any trace of a scout outside."

"Fair enough. Now what is it you want?" A brisk note of impatience had come into the man's voice.

"Information. Shaner told me you would be the only man in Latigo I should trust."

"And how am I to know that I should trust you? Anyone might have picked up that card of Shaner's, you know. It could be a forgery or even a real message stolen from the real messenger. You'd better tell me enough about the situation so I'll be sure of you."

McCall had a feeling that Stallcup was not too pleased at having things work out this way, but he ignored the guarded hostility. "A fair enough doubt," he observed. "Here's my yarn. You wrote to Shaner about two weeks ago, confidentially, telling him that your ore shipments had been subject to a lot of strange attention. You couldn't understand why your business was being

75

watched but you were certain that someone was spying both on the mines and your transportation work. You had reported it to the authorities here in Latigo Pass but they hadn't been able to learn a thing. You wrote to Shaner because you were worried. It didn't shape up like any kind of a hijacking game, but you could not be sure about it. There didn't seem to be anything off-color among the workmen, either at the mines or on the wagons, but you felt sure something was wrong. You asked for confidential help and I'm it."

"Then why didn't you look me up when you first came to town?" This time the question was sharper. McCall decided that Stallcup didn't like the implication that he was being by-passed.

"I wanted to have a look at things before I took any chances of having people connect me with you."

"All right. I suppose you know what you're doing."

"Thanks. Now what can you add to the story that Shaner gave me? Anything happen since your letter to him?"

"A little. The snooping is still a complete mystery, however. We can't put our fingers on a thing and we've never been able to spot any of the men involved. At least not since the incident I reported in my second letter. You know about that, I suppose?"

"No. Shaner mentioned only one letter. What happened?"

"One of our ore trains was held up."

"Looted?"

"No. That's the crazy part of it. A train of six wagons was stopped two miles south of Latigo last week. Two masked men got the drop on our guards. One of them held our men under his gun while the other fellow searched every guard and teamster in the outfit. They didn't take a thing, just rode away empty handed except for the captured guns, which they politely left on the trail a half mile ahead of the train. I'd think it was some kind of fool joke if it didn't happen to be so annoying."

"You reported to the authorities?"

"Of course. I took it up with Mayor Estler and he suggested that we bring Sheriff Brodheiser in on it. The sheriff does not get to Latigo Pass very often; he has to handle parts of the country where the law isn't so well regarded as it is here in Latigo. He came over, however, making a pretty thorough investigation—but with no more success than Doyle had reported."

"Did you get a good description of the holdup men?"

Stallcup laughed shortly. "A description that would fit almost anybody. Two men of medium build and medium height, both in ordinary range clothes. Neither of them said a word except in evidently disguised tones. My men thought they were strangers to Latigo Pass."

McCall doubted that point. Strangers would not have bothered to disguise their voices. He did not mention the idea, though. Instead he asked, "Did Shaner write you about the business at the stamp mill?"

"No. What's that all about?"

"We don't know exactly, but maybe it ties up with the local matter. For the past three weeks Apache's shipments have been checked at the mills by federal officers. They won't tell anyone what they're after but they're keeping a mighty close watch on every batch of ore."

"And you think there's a connection between that matter and our local mystery?"

"I'm here to find out."

"What's this I hear about your being an old resident of this country?" The question was abrupt enough so that McCall realized that it was the explanation of Stallcup's doubts. The mining official had probably heard some pretty wild tales about Larry McCall.

"That's why I was picked for the job. I've done other investigation work for Shaner since I lost my interest in show business and he knew that this country used to be my home. So he sent for me, figuring that the local angle would give me a good plausible reason to appear in town. Unfortunately for me the local part seems to have involved me in an added bit of trouble."

He sketched in the main events of the past two days, stressing the way Doyle and his crowd had displayed worry over the Wapitis. Stallcup grumbled uneasily.

"I don't like the sound of that. We'll need Doyle with us if this thing breaks badly, and you're squarely on the wrong side of him."

"You can't figure on Doyle if he's ridin' with the outlaw crowd."

"Two different matters· entirely," Stallcup snapped. "I suppose you've run onto something back there in the crags, perhaps the route by which stolen beef is worked into the border country. I have reason to believe that such a trade exists, as I was about to explain. I don't even doubt that Ross Doyle knows about the game and is taking a profit from it—but I don't believe that it has anything to do with our problem. To my way of thinking you have ruined your usefulness to Apache by letting yourself get involved in another matter."

"But suppose there's a connection?"

"I still don't believe it. Your rustlers seem interested only in the hills north of the pass. Our trouble has been entirely centered in the south."

"I still think there's a connection. There are just too many people involved in this deal for it to be a two-bit rustling job."

"Maybe the rustling is not such a small game as you seem to think. I've been getting mighty suspicious of a fellow named Trondell who has been supplying both the town slaughter house and the mine commissary with beef."

"Ears Trondell?"

"That's the man. Do you know him?"

"We met—informally."

The irony was lost on Stallcup. He went on quickly.

"He has been selling us beef for some months, and I never could figure him out as a simple cattle dealer. Then our commissary chief came to me with the story that his skinners had noticed something funny about the brands on the cattle they were getting. They were never the brands of any outfits near here. In fact, they were completely unknown to any of our men."

"You did something about it?"

"Not until recently. We understood that a dealer might handle many brands but the whole thing looked so funny that I ordered a complete check of the hides, inside and out. Yesterday I was informed that every cow we buy is probably stolen. The brands have all been altered."

"Any idea what the original markings were?"

"We haven't gone that far yet. I've wired Sheriff Brodheiser to take charge of the case and I'm having my men bring me a tally of all brands still available for comparison."

"You think the sheriff is honest—or is he like Doyle?"

"I think he's honest; but then I trusted Doyle."

"When do you expect Brodheiser?"

"Any time. Tomorrow, perhaps."

"Stall him off a bit, if you can. I need time to work out a couple of points."

Stallcup seemed to stiffen a little. "I'm afraid that will be out of the question. I'll put the matter before him and the rest will be up to him. You'll have to remember that you're the one who complicated this mess—not me."

"We won't argue about that. Just give me a chance to take action before this thing gets complicated. I've got Doyle to buck now, and I'm not anxious to take on some other doubtful lawman."

"And I'm not even sure I agree with you on Doyle. So far as the company is concerned he's doing all right. He keeps the town in order and saves us a lot of trouble. Before he cleaned things up we lost men every pay day.

There were fights, knifings and all the rest of it. Now we're pretty free of that sort of thing, and I'll give Doyle full credit. Maybe he's taking graft from cattle thieves but I've got an idea you're imagining a good portion of the blame you put on him."

"I guess this is where we quit," McCall said briefly. "I'll not try to prove a case on Doyle now. All I ask is that you keep quiet about this talk."

"I don't need that advice," Stallcup said stiffly. "I know my duty—and it is not concerned with rustling other than to notify the proper authorities."

"Then I'll give you some different advice," McCall told him grimly. "Don't leave here for quite some time after I go. It won't be healthy for you if your good friend Doyle knows that you've been talking to me. You'd better believe that."

He slipped out of the front door without further words, standing motionless in the night for several seconds before starting around toward the lane which led to the rear. In that interval his ear caught the stealthy scrape of a boot heel in the alley on the opposite side of the office. Evidently the meeting had been observed in spite of precautions. He did not think the spy could have learned much, though; the talk had been kept too low.

The six-gun was in his hand as he swung into the darkness. One spy might mean another, and he knew that from now on he could expect nothing but violence. Once he thought he heard running footsteps ahead of him but the sound died as he stopped to listen, and nothing else came to disturb his cautious progress toward the Silver Strike.

His next move was obvious now, even though he knew that it would not be an easy one to make. He had to get back to the Wapitis. Every answer seemed to depend on knowing where that rustler canyon led. If it turned southward, crossing the rail line and ending somewhere in the neighborhood of the Apache mines, he thought he knew what to do. Until he could prove that he was stuck.

He worked toward the hotel, using every precaution as he neared the danger zone. There was still a lot of noise in the street but he could detect no new note in it. Apparently there had been nothing in the way of a new development, probably because Doyle had not yet completed his plans. Suddenly he turned aside and eased himself in along the side of the saloon where he had seen Doyle going with Trondell and Olson. It was a risky move but he knew that he would have to gamble somewhere, and it seemed like a good bet to make a play for some information.

The saloon seemed to be doing a tremendous business and McCall almost held his breath as he approached a back window. Shouting men seemed to be almost at his elbow, and after the darkness of the lane he felt quite conspicuous in the partially relieved gloom. Common sense told him, however, that he was moving in shadow and, barring accidents, would not be seen. Still it was nervous work, snooping there and searching for a window through which he might pick up some word or other.

Twice he listened to nothing but the loud talk of celebrating miners, but then he struck pay dirt. The next window was directly behind a table where Doyle, Trondell and Wells were sitting. Just as McCall looked in they were approached by a tall, suave-looking Mexican in native garb. The fellow who had talked with Zellers behind the hotel, without a doubt.

His careful speech confirmed the guess. "I do not find Señor Jake," he announced flatly. "I look careful but he ees not there."

Doyle stood up, cursing under his breath. "That damned polecat! If he's let the redhead rawhide him again I'll kill the yella son! Ears! Git over to Langan's place and tell Ten-spot to keep his eyes open. McCall will likely head for Langan's if he's loose. Manuel, yuh better come with me. We got to move fast."

McCall faded into the darkness as the quartet left the saloon hurriedly. The hunt was on. Getting out of Latigo Pass tonight was going to be a man's size job.

9

There had been a subtle alteration in the sound of Latigo's revelry when McCall slipped back into the darkness. Or so it seemed to his listening ears. He thought he could detect a slackening in the tempo of excitement as well as a lessening of the noise itself, as though the drunken miners had stopped their celebration to listen. He could imagine the whispered questions as men watched the marshal's actions. Definitely the town was building up pressure for an explosion.

He shook his head impatiently, calling it imagination. Latigo Pass was not so responsive to the moods of its mountainous marshal. Better to stop dreaming things and pay attention to that lantern which was bobbing around in the backyard of the Silver Strike Hotel. Sooner or later they would find the helpless Jake Zellers —and then the steam pressure would really go up!

He made a wide detour so as to avoid the hotel and to cross the street at a spot beyond the center of raucous activity. Even then there would be three major risks to assume before he could hope to get out of Latigo Pass. He had to cross the railroad tracks, an open space which would certainly be guarded, he had to dodge the man at the livery stable, and he had to offer Shorty Langan his full confidence. Even though he thought he could trust Shorty he had not yet been willing to go so far, but now he knew there was no alternative. From now on he would be quite dependent upon the little man and a completely discreet policy would be out of the question. Shorty would have to have the facts, both for his own good and for McCall's.

The first hazard almost proved to be the last one. He emerged into the street just in time to be accosted by a tall figure whose conical hat made a distinguishing silhouette against the lights of the town. The Mexican started to speak, apparently confident that he was talking to one of his own crowd. Then, abruptly he broke off and started some sort of rapid movement. McCall was too fast for him. The redhead had seized his opportunity eagerly, stepping in as the Mexican opened his lips to speak. After that it was too late for him to see his mistake. McCall's borrowed gun slammed hard against the side of Manuel's head and there was a quick repetition of the Zellers drama.

It was easier to make the Mexican into a helpless bundle. The serape and a gaudy sash provided ample materials and within a matter of minutes McCall had tucked his man away into an alley between two adobe shacks. Then he headed boldly out across the railroad. It wasn't likely that there would be another guard so close at hand.

But there was. He had just stepped across the rails when a husky voice challenged sharply, "Hold up there! Where're yuh headin', pilgrim?"

The darkness was so complete that McCall could not see even an outline of the speaker so he took the bold course. Imitating the precise tones of the Mexican he hissed a reply. "I go to spik weeth Señor Ten-spot. He ees at the stable, no?"

"Oh! It's Manuel, hey? Yeah, Ten-spot's over there, all right, but Ears was just talkin' to him. He'll be watchin' right sharp so look out he don't plug yuh. He's apt to shoot first and ask questions later."

"I weel be careful. He ees behind the stable, no?"

83

"No is right. He's hunkered down in the doorway of the little adobe on the west side o' Langan's place."

"*Gracias*. I find heem."

"Yuh'll find Ten-spot, all right," the man called grimly after him as McCall faded across toward the north side. "But will they find Jake? I'm bettin' that waddie is a gone goslin."

The uneasiness in the man's voice was both a warning and a suggestion. Doyle's followers were getting nervous enough to be really dangerous. Every man's finger would be tense on a trigger, and any sudden move was likely to bring a bullet. On the other hand it might be possible to play upon this very nervousness. The disappearance of Jake Zellers had left them with a healthy respect for the prowess of the stranger who had already won fast victories over Trondell, Zellers and Ott. Maybe the fact could be turned to some account.

McCall didn't know just what use he could make of the idea but he did know that the time for delay had passed. Timid moves had to be forgotten. Only boldness would serve now. He circled again, approaching the stable from the west so as to be in shadow to the guard who had been so conveniently spotted for him. Using the corner of the adobe shack as cover he gambled once more on his ability to mimic the tall Mexican.

"Señor Ten-spot!"

A startled grunt came clearly, followed by the click of a hammer being drawn back to full cock. McCall followed up the surprise promptly, trying to keep the guard from collecting his wits. "I come to guard the back of the stable, *compadre*. You weel remember I am there, please. Do not be hasty to shoot eef I come to you again. *Comprende?*"

"I gotcha, Manuel." The fellow's tone carried a note of relief that was almost comic. Apparently he shared the other man's dread of contact with the swift-moving enemy. McCall was almost sorry that he could not

84

follow up the ruse and make a finished job of this guard. It would be rather easy, he thought, but it would not be sound tactics. An attack on Ten-spot would be discovered too promptly and would point squarely to Langan's place as a center of interest. More subtle craft was going to be required.

He slid away in the blackness before Ten-spot could say any more, making his way to a clump of mesquite about a hundred feet directly in the rear of the adobe. Then he masked his gun carefully to conceal the flash from possible observation and fired one shot. Almost in the same split second he yelled, "Ten-spot! Queek!" By the time the echoes died away he was rounding the east side of the stable.

He could hear the guard's running feet on the far side of the building while somewhere in the middle distance another man yelled excitedly. Only those two sounds rose above the muffled clamor of the town and then he was hustling into the stable, his nostrils catching the reek of Shorty Langan's strong tobacco.

The stableman blurted an astonished question as McCall appeared in the yellow lamplight for just the instant required to pass the doorway. "What's goin' on, Larry? Who's . . .?"

McCall dodged out of the light. "Get outside there and ask plenty of questions, Shorty. Somebody will be along in a second or two. Raise a lot of fuss."

Langan seemed to understand. "Got 'em after ye, eh?" he remarked, sidling through the doorway. "I figgered ye would."

"Don't figure. Get out there and holler a bit!"

"Right. Better climb over the hay pile. There's a trap door in the wall behind it if things git too hot."

Running footsteps in the near distance warned McCall to move promptly. He made a running dive at the hay pile which filled a rear corner of the stable, sliding over its top to take refuge in a cranny where the hay

85

did not quite fill the angle. A swift motion or two brought the hay across over his head and then he fumbled around to find the loose-fitting wooden window which Langan had mentioned. With his ear to the opening he could hear hurrying sounds from the rear while at the same time he caught the opening salvo of loud questions from Shorty Langan out front. Someone had arrived and Shorty was giving them an earful.

The new arrivals separated quickly and McCall could hear a voice shouting questions at Ten-spot. The result was a fast conference which pleased the listener considerably. Ten-spot was insisting that Manuel must have spotted McCall and was even now engaged in chasing him. The shot had been either the opening of the pursuit or a signal from the Mexican. The other man agreed without much argument, and the two of them hurried back to join the man who was talking to Langan. McCall could only hope that the theory would be accepted. It might draw them away from the stable and give him a chance to make a getaway.

Part of the talk was repeated at the front of the building, interrupting Shorty's querulous demands to know what in tarnation was goin' on. Ten-spot was insistent now, apparently impressed by his own reconstruction of what he had heard. "The redhead musta been tryin' to sneak a bronc outa here. Manuel spotted him. Yuh'd better start circlin' to see if mebbe the Mex needs help. That McCall's a bad hombre, yuh know."

The rest of the conversation was in whispers but it ended with another rush of footsteps as two men hurried away. Then two other men moved more slowly into the stable.

"Then yuh're plumb certain yuh ain't seen McCall since he drifted in at dusk?" a voice asked. It was a new voice to McCall, so he decided that the guard had been changed, that Ten-spot had been sent to hunt for Manuel.

Langan's reply sounded aggrieved. "Why shouldn't I be certain? I ain't runnin' no home fer homeless outlaws! Anyway, Ten-spot would ha' seen him if he'd come around. I heard what he said—and I ain't likin' it none. Guardin' my place like I was up to somethin' crooked!"

The other man seemed anxious to placate the irate stableman. "Nobody's accusin' yuh of nothin', Shorty. We jest know yuh hired a bronc to that jasper the other day, and it seemed likely he mighta come back here."

"Well, he didn't!"

"Don't git proddy. Did yuh figure he'd be ridin' out again?"

"He didn't say nothin' to me about it."

"How're yuh guessin'?"

"I ain't got no call to guess. When he hired that first bronc he talked like he'd be gone a week, but he was back next day. Mebbe he's had a bellyful."

"He'll git one—a bellyful o' lead. Shorty, are yuh sure that hombre is Larry McCall?"

"Dang right! I knew him when he was the hell-raisin'est young sidewinder in these here parts."

"Ever know him to be hooked up with the Gov'-ment?"

"Nope. He left here and went into some kind o' show business. Now he's back. That's all I know."

There was a pause and then the stranger spoke again, soothingly. "Mebbe it ain't as bad as we think, but Doyle shore wants to find out what that polecat's up to. Yuh'd be doin' the marshal a favor if yuh make shore McCall don't git no bronc out yore string—if he should happen to turn up and ask fer one."

"Rentin' broncs is my business," Langan bristled. "I'll run my own show!"

"All right, all right! Don't git so proddy about everything a man says to yuh. I'm just . . ."

The declaration broke off short as a gunshot boomed

from somewhere in Latigo. Immediately Ten-spot's voice howled an alarm. "Manuel's got 'im, I bet. Come on, Curly!"

The man who had been talking to Langan rushed out of the stable, shouting a reply. Evidently he had a cooler head than some of the others of his crew, just as he had displayed better diplomacy in talking to Shorty, for he yelled a quick order at Ten-spot.

"Come back here, Ten-spot! We'll change plans. Pronto!"

McCall could hear some low-voiced wrangling at the front of the stable as Ten-spot returned, then the voices moved to the rear of the stable and he could hear the conversation clearly through the trap door.

"I know how it sounds," Curly was saying, "but yuh can't always tell. Mebbe it was Manuel and mebbe it wasn't. Anyway, yuh gotta stick on the job here. I'll slip back here and let yuh know what happened."

"Don't poke along; I'm gittin' curious," Ten-spot grumbled. "Yuh think Langan's helpin' this McCall jigger?"

"It don't look like it to me, but keep yuhr eyes and ears open. If McCall shows up yuh better blast him right away without askin' questions. Then hightail outa town. We'll hang the killin' on Langan if we can; if we can't we'll find some other angle. Keep awake; the jigger's a tough nut."

"I reckon he's fixed now. I'm bettin' Manuel got him."

"Keep yuhr eyes open anyhow. I'll let yuh know what's what in town."

There was the sound of retreating footsteps and then Ten-spot moved away, taking up his guard post in front of the adobe once more. It suited McCall well enough; now he could talk a bit with Shorty Langan.

He crawled quietly over the hay pile, keeping out of the lantern's rays as he moved across to where Langan was again smoking quietly. The little man could not be

88

sure of the location of the guard so he was putting on a pretty good act.

"One guard in front of the place next door," McCall told him in a whisper. "I'm going to make a break for it. Can you get a good bronc saddled and ready without giving the show away?"

Langan nodded. "I kin do it—but ye'll have the whole outfit on yer tail if yuh ride outa town now."

"Can't help it. Better an open chase than being trapped here. Throw a hull on the toughest bronc you've got, and fix me up about two days' grub. If I can't get finished and be back here in two days, I won't be coming."

Langan nodded and drifted away, disappearing into another part of the stable and muttering soothingly to a horse as he began the task he had accepted. McCall slid back into a shadow to wait, letting his thoughts run to the problem ahead of him. He had to get out of Latigo Pass in order to trace that canyon where the rustler trail ran. It was more than a rustler trail, he felt certain, but he was not yet sure what he expected to find there. Somehow the whole arrangement must fit in with the odd surveillance of mine wagons, and he would have to get at the real facts if he hoped to break up the gang. And he had to break it up. No longer would there be any doubt on that score. Either he smashed the whole outfit, or they would kill him.

Only briefly did he consider that he might be making a bad guess in heading toward the Wapitis. On the surface it might seem foolish to strike northward on the trail of a mystery which centered around the mines to the south of Latigo, but he was convinced that the rustler trail would connect the two areas. That canyon in the Wapitis was the key to the whole riddle and a search of the canyon seemed like the only way to solve the riddle.

One thing bothered him more than he cared to admit.

He hated to believe that Jim Tanner was implicated in the game, but it seemed certain that the old man must know something of what was going on. He had let Glennister do the talking on the subject of the rustlers' canyon but he was staying strictly away from it, a fact which hinted that he was obeying outlaw orders.

That conclusion made McCall realize how much he had come to value his new plans for a return to K-Bar. Only a few days ago there had been simply a vague interest in seeing the place again; now he knew that a return had come to mean a great deal. It was another good reason why he had to smash the outlaw crowd.

He grinned wryly in the darkness as he recognized the double quality to that new ambition. One look at the valley behind the crags had aroused a definite nostalgia, but there was another reason why K-Bar had seemed inviting, a reason which he recalled in terms of soft brown hair and a smooth oval face which was pleasant even behind a frown. He could only hope that it wasn't going to be necessary to implicate Helen Tanner's father in this business of cracking down on rustlers.

Langan slipped back into view again, idling past McCall and speaking without any indication that he was aware of another person near him. "Bronc's ready, Larry. What next?" He paused to throw a few wisps of hay to the top of the pile, using the action to cover the brief conversation.

"Better wander out again," McCall whispered. "There's a guard next door, I know, but I'd like to be sure that he's alone. See what you can make out."

Shorty moved away silently, strolling out into the night as though for an evening stretch. McCall waited silently. No point in moving around while there was a chance that some other guard might be peering into the place. He moved quickly, however, as a patter of talk broke out near the front door. Shorty had engaged Ten-spot in conversation just as a messenger arrived from town.

"Who killed him?" Ten-spot asked quickly.

"Doyle ain't found out yet. All we know is that a miner heard the shot and found him layin' in the dirt alongside his office! We're layin' odds on McCall as the killer."

"Say! That's right!" Ten-spot seemed elated at his own understanding. "They had a brawl the other night, didn't they? Now we really got somethin' on that polecat."

"How d'ye figure?" Langan interrupted. "McCall beat this feller Ott so it woulda been Ott who was tryin' to git square. McCall didn't have no reason to take it out on Ott. Better find a new idea."

"This one's good enough for us," the newcomer stated definitely. "Marshal Doyle's orders are to bring him in—dead or alive. Any sign of him around, Ten-spot?"

"Not a speck. I still figure Manuel's runnin' him hard somewhere. Seems queer yuh can't git on the Mex's trail."

The rest of the talk was valueless to McCall, but he had heard enough to let him know that the noose was tightening on his neck. Now the outlaw crowd could play at being lawmen. Someone had shot Henderson Ott, and McCall was known to have quarreled with Ott. That dead or alive order would mean only one thing to Doyle's men.

He could hear movements outside and presently knew that the messenger had returned across the tracks toward the town. Then Shorty Langan came in, motioning for him to stay back in the darkness. The liveryman went through elaborate motions of picking up bits of equipment and hanging them on hooks, using the activity as a mask for his conversation with McCall. "One man outside, and he's gone around to the back. Ye heard the report, I reckon?"

McCall nodded. "They're making the place kinda hot for me. Are you sure that other jasper didn't stay?"

"Sure. He's on his way back to town. Ten-spot's goin' to stick close to the back corner of the stable in case Manuel comes back from that direction. Maybe ye kin make it if we ease the pony to the door right quiet."

McCall shook his head. "That won't do. It would put them on your neck in a hurry, and I don't want that. Neither do I want quite so prompt a chase. I've got to silence our friend Ten-spot."

"It's a big risk. He's primed to shoot first, ye know."

"Everything's a risk in this business. Bustle around and make some noise in here. I want to get as close to him as I can before I play my cards."

"Luck," Shorty said briefly. "Ye'll need it."

The redhead grinned mirthlessly and eased himself out of the big front door. It was almost too much to hope that Ten-spot would be as easy a victim as Zellers and the Mexican.

10

He stuck close to the wall of the stable, working around by way of the east side until he could see the whole expanse of the rear wall. It was easy to find the guard. Ten-spot was lounging at the northwest corner of the building, evidently watching the alley and the western approaches to the stable. He was smoking a cigarette, keeping it cupped in concealing hands which still permitted its intermittent flare to outline his head and shoulders to the watcher. McCall took a half dozen cautious steps toward him, then spoke suddenly, his voice low but harsh.

"Ten-spot, you damned fool! Knock off that smokin'! Wanta give yerself away?"

There was a startled grunt and a streak of fire as the cigarette went to the ground to be crushed underfoot. "What the hell!" Ten-spot managed to mutter, his caution overcome by guilty confusion. "I was keepin' it covered with my hands."

"Fine lot o' good that was doin'," McCall growled, striding boldly toward the guard. "It showed up like a lantern on a pole. Nacherly yuh ain't seen nothin' with that lighthouse goin'. Or did yuh?"

"Ain't seen hide nor hair o' . . ."

That was enough. Ten-spot's sense of guilt had been too much for his mental processes. He had been so busy explaining the ill-advised cigarette that he had forgotten his caution. The lapse had been only a matter of seconds but the interval had been long enough for McCall's purpose. As soon as he was within striking distance he let fly with the same jolting right that had twice stunned Jake Zellers. It was equally effective against Ten-spot. The fellow went down with just a single grunt, and then McCall was on him with a bound making certain that it was indeed a knockout. Ten-spot's own belt and bandanna served as bonds and gag, the chore being accomplished with much speed. A matter of practice, McCall told himself with a half smile.

He took Ten-spot's gun and gun belt, slinging the outfit on his own lean hips as he started toward the front of the stable once more. There was no sound of any other person in the vicinity, so he went in without hesitation to find Shorty standing there with his gnarled fist on the bridle of a big rangy sorrel. He grinned amiably at McCall and asked, "Git him?"

"You bet. He's tied up back in the shadows but I'll move him away when I go. I don't want anything pointing to you in this mess."

"Don't worry about me. I do enough worryin' about myself."

McCall laughed at the little man's quizzical humor but

spoke briskly. "I'm going to pick up that jigger and dump him along the trail a short distance out of town. It'll keep them from finding him tonight and maybe help to keep them all in a pucker. They're spooked up now over the way their boys keep disappearing so this oughta help a mite. Give me as long as you think is safe, then hustle down the street and make a loud squawk to Doyle. Tell him a masked man held you up and stole a horse. Describe the masked man as looking like Ten-spot."

Langan chuckled briefly but shook his head. "That won't be good enough, Larry. As soon as they know ye've got a bronc they'll be on yer tail. Better let 'em find it out for theirselves."

"Fifteen minutes will be enough for me. I want you to stay in the clear."

"Don't fuss about me. I'm used to trouble. Earth's but a doggone desert dreary; heaven's where I hang up my saddle."

"Now you're sounding like yourself. And don't think I'm worrying about your worthless hide. I'm just figuring I might need you again, and you'll be a lot more valuable to me if the Doyle outfit doesn't know you're helping me."

"I mighta knowed it was somethin' like that. I'll give ye twenty minutes unless I hear somebody headin' this way."

"Right. But don't wait too long."

McCall swung into the saddle and urged the sorrel out into the darkness. "Another thing," he called over his shoulder. "If I don't get back with your disreputable old nag you can send your bill to the Apache Mining Company. They'll pay it—if you don't try to charge them for a real horse."

"Git!" Shorty hissed. "And don't be insultin' General Beauregard!"

McCall chuckled and eased the pony around the

corner of the stable to where Ten-spot still lay inert. The man stirred uneasily as McCall hoisted him to the pony's back but there was no particular trouble about it. A minute later the horse was walking out of town, heading toward the Wapitis.

There was no sound of any alarm and presently Mc-Call pulled up to unload his prisoner. He knew that Ten-spot was conscious now, but he pretended to be unaware of it. As though talking to himself he muttered, "We'll just leave him out here on this side o' town, I reckon. It'll make it look like I'm headed north."

Ten-spot suddenly ceased his squirming and McCall decided that the man was swallowing the bait. It wouldn't be a ruse of any permanent value, he knew, but any little bit of help would be worth while. The evening's successes had been based entirely on catching the enemy unprepared—and that would not be possible any longer. From now on it would be a fight against long odds.

He eased the sorrel across the alkali flats until he felt that he was out of hearing for any listeners in Latigo Pass, then he gave the pony a heel and dashed for the Wapiti slope. Finding the trail up the mountain was going to be something of a chore in the darkness, but he thought he would be able to make it. Olson hadn't done too badly so Larry McCall ought to fare as well.

He tried to plan as he picked his way through the mesquite clumps but it was difficult for his thoughts to reach beyond the single conclusion that the rustler canyon connected with the mining region south of the rail line. That fact must be the key point of the whole puzzle, but he could not make any real guess as to what that key would unlock.

Somewhat less clearly he knew that his plans would have to include a showdown with the folks at K-Bar. He had to know whether Jim Tanner was working with Walt Glennister or was being hoodwinked by him. One way or another Glennister was a problem to be faced. The surly rider had already spilled the beans to the rustler gang and must be reckoned as a dangerous enemy.

It left the question of K-Bar's stock losses pretty much in doubt. If Tanner was a crook the cattle losses were probably faked. If Tanner was honest it seemed reasonable to believe that Glennister was taking an active hand in the rustling. The latter alternative seemed more credible, McCall thought, hoping that he was not letting sentiment warp his thinking. He did not want to find the Tanners involved, but he still knew nothing that would eliminate the possibility.

The night turned colder as he climbed, its stillness in sharp contrast to the turmoil of his thoughts and of the town he had left behind. Once he paused at a turn of the trail, listening intently for sounds of pursuit on the long slope in his rear but nothing came to disturb the serenity of the night. Apparently his escape had not yet brought action from the worried gang which surrounded Marshal Ross Doyle. Maybe they would not take a chance of pursuit until they were able to locate their missing companion.

Dawn was breaking clear and chill over the crags when he leveled off into the canyon which led to the Devil's Cockpit. He paused then, examining the trail in the gray light to make certain that no one had preceded him during the night. The canyon floor indicated nothing more recent than his own passage in the opposite direction but he went ahead with caution, remembering that Ears Trondell had ridden into Latigo from some part of this country. It seemed fair to assume that Trondell had left companions somewhere in the canyons, companions who might be awaiting his return somewhere ahead. It would not be healthy to stumble into that kind of reception.

With the thought in mind he was pretty careful with

96

his movements as he approached the intersection, a caution which paid off promptly. Dismounting just short of the last canyon bend he went forward afoot and was rewarded by the sight of four riders hazing a small bunch of cattle into the eastern canyon. Even at the distance he could see that several different brands were represented in the lot, three or four K-Bars included.

He watched while the shouting riders pushed the beef out of sight into the canyon. Then one man cut away from the other herders and picketed his bronc in a clump of pines. With quick, efficient movements he cut pine boughs and proceeded to sweep that portion of the ground where loose dirt might carry the story of the herd's passage. McCall squinted grimly at the performance, aware that this must be a well-practiced stunt. Olson had done it well and now another rider was doing it.

He decided that it was significant that the rustler did not attempt to blot any part of the trail except the actual crossing of the rustler route and the trail to K-Bar. The blind was directed squarely at Larry McCall. Evidently these men had not heard from their cohorts in Latigo Pass or they would not be taking such pains. Doyle and his gunmen could have told them that the time for fooling McCall was past. Deception was a dead issue; McCall was to be treated with more direct methods.

The trail blotter disposed of his pine boughs behind some piled boulders and remounted, riding hard into the east canyon on the trail of the rustled beef. They were leaving no guard at the intersection, McCall decided. None of the men had shown any sign of throwing a farewell salute toward the rimrock, a gesture which certainly would have come had there been a man up there. That ought to be a help.

He went back to the waiting sorrel, rubbing the bronc's nose thoughtfully before climbing into the saddle. "Looks like we change our plans, Bo," he said. "That herd won't move too fast and we might find something right interesting if we do a bit of back-trailing."

The pony threw his head high and McCall laughed. "Going to be fancy, are you? I suppose back-trailing is no job for General Beauregard. Too bad. I'd have had Shorty give me a Forrest or a Jeb Stuart if I'd known what kind of a job this was going to be."

He vaulted into the saddle and sent the animal briskly into the tumbled little valley, risking a bullet with complete boldness. Nothing happened and he swung quickly across to the mouth of the east canyon, glancing briefly at the newly swept sand at the edge of the canyon walls. In another hour the morning breezes would have completely smoothed away all signs of the herd's passage.

It was only when he entered the north canyon that he took time to study the ground more intently. There were tracks there, all right, but not enough to account for the size of the herd he had seen. Perhaps a dozen head of K-Bar steers had been driven south along the Latigo-K-Bar trail, evidently joining a larger bunch of rustled cattle coming in from the west. He looked for pony tracks returning to K-Bar but could find none. The men who had brought the K-Bar beef had stayed with the main herd.

He hesitated briefly, then sent the sorrel on to the north. There would be time later to trace that herd down the rustler canyon. He didn't want to come upon them too soon, and he felt that he could use the time more profitably to make a second visit to K-Bar. Maybe this time he could get a better line on where the Tanners stood in this dirty business.

It was not yet mid-morning when he saw the green slopes of K-Bar valley again. After the sheer rocks of the badlands there was something a little startling about that verdant spot and he felt the same thrill which he had known earlier. Even without the contrast of the barren crags to the south this valley would be beautiful. After the wilderness of granite behind him it was almost startling in its peacefulness.

A trickle of smoke climbed into the still air from the ranch house but this was not the point to attract attention. McCall's quick eye was caught by the sight of two riders coming toward him across the shoulder of the mountain. Jim Tanner and Walt Glennister should be out on the range at this time of day but here they were, heading toward the canyon trail along the upper bench.

He knew what it meant without waiting to ask. They were trailing the stolen cattle. He could see the sign easily enough and knew that the rustled beef had been driven across this way so as to avoid passing close to the ranch house, probably during the early hours of the previous evening. To all intents and purposes both Tanner and Glennister were honestly worried so McCall decided to keep his suspicions to himself.

"How many did you lose this time?" he asked Tanner abruptly as he pulled up in front of the two men.

Tanner's lined face looked drawn and tired. "Eleven head. Prime steers. Seen 'em?"

"I reckon so. The trail leads south and I saw some cattle back there that looked like stolen stock to me. When did you lose 'em?"

Tanner ignored the question. "Who had 'em?" he snapped. "And why didn't ye do somethin' about it?"

"Several reasons," McCall told him calmly. "In the first place I was a little curious about so small a number being taken. In the second place I'm no fool. A man with any sense doesn't pick a fight with a rustler over eleven head of cattle."

Glennister sneered audibly. "And then mebbe yuh didn't want to make trouble fer yer friends," he suggested. "It seems mighty queer that yuh know so danged much about it."

"You'd think it queerer than that if you only knew how much I do know about it," McCall told him grimly. "Maybe this bit of bad judgment on the part of the rustlers is going to be the break I've been looking for."

He watched Glennister as he spoke, aware that the fellow was having a hard time keeping his face under control. Either he was dismayed at seeing McCall still alive, or he was pretty badly shaken to realize that the rustlers had been spotted so promptly. McCall had a notion that there was a little of both behind that obvious concern.

Tanner elected to pass up both hints. "Where was they headed?" he asked.

"Into a canyon toward the east. Do you know where this trail behind me breaks out into a little opening full of rocks?"

"Sure."

"Right there. The rustlers were using what I always thought was a blind cut next to where the Latigo trail opens out of the badlands. It shouldn't be hard to trail them if somebody doesn't put them wise to the fact that they've been spotted." He glanced at Walt Glennister as he spoke, getting a quick rise from the surly one.

"Meaning who?"

"I didn't say—but I do know that the thieves have been getting help from someone." He didn't explain further, leaving the glowering rider to squirm uneasily. "Where were these cattle bedded before the rustlers picked 'em up?"

"That's the queer part," Tanner growled. "I didn't know any of our beef was so close in toward the mountains but we found a trail all right. This bunch was bedded right under the break of the crag country and the thieves picked 'em up there."

"Mighty convenient, I'd say," McCall commented. "Any idea how they happened to be there?"

The old man glanced uneasily at Glennister. "I was doin' a few chores around the corral yesterday afternoon. Walt was the last one in from the range and he told me the steers was all out in the lower valley."

"And so they was!" Glennister snarled, his face showing red under the heavy tan. "If yuh're hintin' that I rounded up beef fer rustlers yuh better start thinkin' all over again. I ain't the one what showed up right on the rustlers' trail, yuh know."

"Save the talk," McCall advised. "Let's ride out and see what the trail shows in the valley."

"We already back-trailed 'em," Tanner volunteered. "Two riders hazed 'em across into the canyon last night, I reckon, and I'm guessin' they musta started early in the evenin'."

"Meaning that the thieves had the beef spotted before dark?"

"It kinda looks that way."

"Did you see anything to hint that the steers were rounded up there for the rustlers to find?"

"I didn't think about that. We just happened to stumble on the place where they'd been bedded so we trailed 'em from there."

"Then suppose we take another look," McCall suggested, his eye on Glennister. "It ought to be interesting."

"Yuh needn't try to shove it off on me," the rider snapped. "I ain't . . ."

"Let's see what the trail shows. After that we'll know more about who's guilty." He made it sound quite mild, but something in his attitude seemed to impress his hearers. Neither of them spoke as they wheeled their broncs and headed back along the trail of the stolen beef.

McCall followed silently. He was beginning to hope that this might be a partial showdown. Unless all the signs were very misleading Jim Tanner was an honest victim while Walt Glennister was really an inside man for the rustler crowd. That was how he had hoped it would be.

11

Still he watched both men carefully. Glennister's sudden docility was a matter for suspicion and it was not yet safe to trust Tanner. The old man might be honest and still be ready to turn on a fellow who had not yet clearly established his own good intentions. The trail was not hard to read as they rode down into the opening beyond the higher bench, even when attention had to be divided between the sign and the silent men ahead. Even before they had reached the lower valley McCall knew that Tanner had interpreted the sign correctly. Two riders had herded eleven steers across this shoulder of mountain, probably in the early hours of the previous evening.

Twenty minutes of easy travel brought them to a sheltered spot where cattle had stood for some little time. Tanner pointed out the tracks where the two rustlers had taken charge and started the little herd toward the canyons. McCall nodded his understanding and swung away, working out toward the main valley to scan the trail where the cattle had come in. It forced him to leave the other two men at his back but he spurred away quickly, putting much distance between himself and the pair before attempting to do much sign reading. Almost immediately he picked up the trail of a rider who had hazed those cattle along only to leave them and slant away toward the creek.

"Over this way, Tanner," he called, watching Glennister carefully. "Here's what I was looking for."

He maintained his careful watch until the other two had approached, then he motioned toward the ground and said, "One rider brought 'em here. Now let's see where he went after he spotted the steers for his crooked pards to pick up."

"Found the trail mighty easy, didn't yuh?" Glennister jeered. "It almost looks like yuh knew where to look."

"What do ye mean by that?" Tanner cut in. "That ain't the first hint ye've passed, Walt. Are ye claimin' McCall played in with the rustlers?"

"Figure it out fer yuhrself," the dark man countered. "Mebbe McCall's the jasper what's been playin' all the hell in this here valley. It could be a real foxy way o' gettin' his hooks on the ranch. If he busts yuh up he could take the place over right easy."

"I've got a lot of answers to that," McCall said, keeping his voice calm. "But we won't argue it now. Just follow this trail and we won't have to do any wild guessing. When we see where this ranny went we'll know pretty well who he was."

For a moment no one moved. McCall's voice took on a bit of an edge as he added, "And you better ride ahead, Walt. I'll feel safer if you and your fancy imagination are in front of me."

"Since when have yuh been givin' the orders around here?" Glennister snarled. "I ain't lettin' no . . ."

He broke off abruptly as McCall's gun appeared as if by magic in a steady right hand. There had been no show of action but the gun was there, its muzzle trained upon Glennister's belly.

"Since right now I'm givin' the orders," McCall told him crisply. "Just mind your manners and nobody will get hurt."

"What's the idea, McCall?" Tanner protested. "I don't like this thing at all. You're . . ."

"I don't like it either," McCall interrupted. "I didn't

like it when this dirty polecat went out of his way to rush over and tell his dirty pals about me the other morning. Up to that time I had a chance to look into this deal with some margin of personal safety. When he finished shooting off his mouth I was bullet bait for the biggest gang of thieves in the southwest. Naturally I'm not feeling too cordial toward the gent that put me in such a jam."

"But I don't understand."

"You will. For now just take my word for it that I'm calling the turns. Let's ride along and see who our cattle spotting friend was. Out ahead, Glennister, and don't get taken with any fatal ideas!"

They pushed on in silence, following the clear sign of a rider who had brought the little bunch of steers to the pick-up spot. Once Tanner glanced understandingly at McCall, but there was no word spoken except when McCall ordered Glennister gruffly back to the trail. The swarthy man had deliberately wandered off, as though trying to lead the trailers astray. It was becoming clear that he did not like the way the sign was lining straight for the K-Bar ranch house.

They climbed the gentle slope along the swift flowing creek and presently saw the house and corrals directly ahead. It was then that McCall snapped a fast order. "Pull up, Walt! Sit tight and get your hands up high! I'm taking your hardware."

The man started to bluster but obeyed orders. Tanner offered a feeble protest but McCall silenced him promptly. "You've seen enough, haven't you? The trail's plenty clear. This is the jigger who spotted those cows for the thieves, just as he probably has spotted dozens of other little bunches before. That's the way this game worked. Small bunches from several different ranches. Never enough at one time for anybody to make a fuss about. Just enough beef to keep a steady and saleable supply going into Latigo Pass."

"But Walt ain't . . ."

"Don't fool yourself. Walt's part of the gang that has been stealing you blind for the last year or so. This time we've got the goods on him. I was willing to bet on it when he made that fast trip over to the cross canyon to let his gang know that I was acting curious about them. Now you've got him dead to rights and we'll keep him out of action for a while and see what makes the rest of the gang tick."

He rode forward cautiously and hooked the forty-five out of Glennister's holster. The dark man shot him a venomous glance but said nothing. Then McCall motioned for him to ride on. "We'll talk business at the house, brother rustler. Get going before I remember how mad I am about that tattletale business."

Helen Tanner met them at the corral. Her eyes were wide with astonishment, but there was indignation mixed with the other emotion as she asked, "What in the world does this mean?"

Glennister shrugged. "Ask the smart boy. He's got a lot of awful humorous ideas—and yuhr pappy seems to think they're plumb comic."

"Climb down," McCall ordered, ignoring the comment and the girl's frown. "We'll give you plenty of chance to do your talking when we're ready. Rustle!"

He waited until the sulky Glennister slid from the saddle and moved a step or two toward the house. Then he halted him with a motion of the gun and dismounted to stand just out of reach. "Take the broncs, will you, Tanner?" he asked. "We'll wait for you."

He waved Glennister toward the house while Tanner put the three ponies into the corral. Helen Tanner watched dubiously, her questioning glance only partly relieved at the way her father was accepting McCall's peremptory orders. Once she caught the redhead's eye but it was only for a moment. She turned away quickly, even before he could shift his attention back to the prisoner.

He motioned Glennister toward a spot along the wall of the cabin. "Stand right there, Walt. We'll let you say your piece as soon as Tanner gets here."

"Who said I wanted to talk?"

"Nobody. But you'd be smart to do it. It's now or later—only later you'll just be one of the gang. Now you've got a chance to put yourself on the right side and make things easier for yourself."

.Glennister sneered again. "Don't give me that kind o' tripe! Yuh know yuh're jest tryin' to cover up fer yuhrself by fixin' to rawhide me. I ain't got nothin' to say." He seemed to be talking for Helen Tanner's benefit, but she did not show any sign of the indignation which he must have been trying to arouse. Her attitude was simply one of concern.

Jim Tanner hurried over then. McCall shot him a quick look and went back to his inquisition of Glennister. "How long have you been teamed up with that rustler outfit, Walt?"

"I tell yuh I don't know nothin' about rustlers."

"Quit stalling!" It was Tanner who interrupted, somewhat to McCall's surprise. "We kin read sign, I reckon. Ye spotted them steers fer the thieves, and I'm thinkin' it wasn't the first time ye done the trick. Talk fast and plenty if ye know what's good fer ye!"

Glennister seemed to sag. "Yuh can't prove a thing," he insisted.

"You're not in court, Walt," McCall warned him. "Maybe we can't produce legal proof that you helped to steal previous bunches of K-Bar beef, but we're plumb sure you did it this time. And I know mighty well you tipped your gang off about me a few days ago. In this particular court that's evidence." He looked sideways at Tanner and inquired, "Do you recall how he left you the other morning when I was here at the ranch?"

"Sure. He started back to the stable to fix a spur that was gettin' loose."

"So he claimed, I suppose. Did you see the spur?"

"No."

"Miss Helen, did you see him come back to the ranch?"

"No."

"And for a very good reason. He never came near the place."

"Sounds reasonable to me," Tanner nodded. "I didn't pick him up again 'til afternoon. He claimed he'd been hazin' some stock outa the mesquite along the mountain."

"What really happened was that he looked back and saw me climbing the western rim of the valley. He knew there was something over there that I wasn't supposed to see—the trail used by his thieving friends in bringing cattle from ranches west of here. So he hustled back through the Latigo canyon to let the gang know that a stranger was interested in them. He passed the word along to a ranny named Olson, and Olson checked up on me pronto. When he found where I'd been studying the rustler sign he lit out for Latigo and told the boss. That's why I've been dodging bushwhack bullets for some hours now. I know too much for the gang's comfort."

"About what?" Helen asked. "And who is this gang you keep talking about?"

"Somethin' he dreamed," Glennister jeered.

McCall ignored him except for the business of keeping him at gun point. "Cattle rustling is their main sideline," he told the girl. "But it's just a sideline, I'm sure. Too many hard characters involved for the small numbers of cattle being stolen. That's one reason why I'm suggesting that Walt can make things easier for himself if he wants to gossip a bit about the other line of business he's been playing shill for. How about it, Glennister?"

"Go to hell!"

"After you, chum. And get rid of that idea you're having about making a break! It shows in your eyes, my friend, and I'm not in a mood to take any chances with you."

Glennister stared sullenly at the ground and McCall went on grimly, "One move and I'm cutting you down. Remember that! Now do you want to talk and save yourself a heap of trouble a little later on?"

"No. And yuh kin still go to hell!" The words were not so crisp now. The man had sagged a bit more since his ambitions about a break had been detected so quickly. Evidently he was beginning to recognize the hopelessness of his situation.

"What will you do with him?" Helen Tanner asked. "From what you say I judge you aren't planning to take him to the law in Latigo Pass."

"The law in Latigo Pass is not what you might call dependable," McCall told her. "We'll have to take care of Walt right here for the present. Anything to keep him out of trouble while I get on the trail of that stolen stock. Do you have anything like a good sturdy room that would serve as temporary calaboose?"

"There's the potato cellar," she suggested. "It has only one door and that's a good sturdy one with a hasp."

"The potato cellar it is," McCall nodded. It brought him a quick satisfaction to find the girl lining up on his side for a change. He was so pleased over it that he ignored the protest her father was about to make. "We'll just make sure Walt don't find himself with too much energy on his hands," he said briskly. "Slide around behind him, Tanner, and take a couple of turns around his wrists. That short hank of rope on the wall there by the corner should do the trick. We'll let a lawman come out and pick him up after we've decided what lawman can be trusted. He doesn't need to think it will be his crooked friend Ross Doyle."

Tanner seemed troubled, but he went over to get the rope as directed. Glennister was slumping dejectedly now, the reference to Doyle having done something to him. McCall waved the girl aside and motioned with his gun for Tanner to close in and do the tying. It was gratifying to realize that the first forward step had been made in untangling the rustler problem, a step which had brought him into alliance with Helen Tanner.

The old man was still frowning as he hastened toward Walt Glennister, the preoccupation and haste combining to betray him. He blundered between McCall and the prisoner. The dark man was swift to take advantage. Coming out of his sullen droop with lightning speed he grabbed Tanner's gun and swung the old man in front of him as a living shield. The move came so fast that McCall had no chance to do a thing about it.

"Now I'm callin' the turns!" Glennister crowed. "Drop that iron, smart boy! Hustle with it or the old man gets a slug in the kidneys. And don't yuh try nothin', Helen! One wrong move outa any of yuh and Pop's a dead pigeon." The click of the old single-action came ominously with the hurried orders.

McCall let his forty-five drop to the ground and Glennister cackled in nervous triumph. "Had it all planned out, didn't yuh? Goin' to do big things, wasn't yuh? All right, I'll play it yuhr own way. The potato cellar it's goin' to be—and don't think I ain't bein' awful easy to let yuh off like that. Lead the way, Helen, and pull up the lid."

The man's jeering voice grated hard on McCall's ears but he knew better than to take open offense. It was just lucky that Glennister had not made recent contact with the Latigo Pass crowd. He wouldn't be allowing Larry McCall to remain alive as a prisoner if he had received orders from Ross Doyle. At any rate there was nothing to do but obey orders while that cocked gun was boring into Jim Tanner's back.

Glennister cackled nastily as he herded his prisoners along, still keeping a tight grip on Tanner's shoulder while he held the old man in front of the gun muzzle. "You go down first, Helen," he ordered when the girl pried up the heavy trap door. "Too bad I ain't got time to stay around and visit with yuh after I leave the boys to cool off in the dark but business is business. Mebbe some other time I'll drop around and make it up to yuh."

She ignored the taunt and went down the steep ladder without a backward glance. McCall could read dread in the brief glance she gave him as she disappeared into the hole and he knew that she was trying to make him understand that he was not to make any wild attempt at a break. While her father was in front of that cocked gun she didn't want anyone to start anything.

She dropped out of sight and Glennister jerked his head toward the opening. "Yuh're next, redhead. Stir yer stumps!" He pushed Tanner forward as he spoke so that all three of them were close to the cellar door at the same time. For just an instant McCall had hopes of making a play, but Glennister snapped an order as though aware of the idea.

"Don't do it, smart boy!" he warned. "One queer shuffle outa yuh and Pop gits it in the back. Step lively. It ain't polite to keep a lady waitin' down there."

McCall controlled himself with an effort. It would have been a real pleasure to try conclusions with this smirking outlaw, but he could not risk Tanner's life. He took another step, preparing to ease himself down the ladder—and then Glennister made his big play.

The gun came around in a vicious arc, its barrel slamming across the back of McCall's head to drive him headlong into the cellar entrance. Almost with the same motion, Glennister tripped Jim Tanner and shoved him hard. To McCall it was a painful, bewildering experience. He knew the shock of iron on the back of his skull and then he knew that he was falling through space into a dank gloominess that smelled of mouldy potatoes. There was a nauseating jolt as he landed partly on his head and partly on one shoulder, then another shock as his twisted body took the blow of Jim Tanner's fall. Mingled with the pain was the sound of a groan from Tanner and a quick little scream from Helen. Then the trap door slammed down and they were left in complete darkness.

12

McCall did not move for what seemed like an hour, but must have been all of a half-minute. The breath had been knocked out of him, his body hurt in a dozen places, and the knob on the back of his head throbbed sickeningly. It would have been a welcome relief to let his reeling senses leave him, but he knew that he had to battle for consciousness. He had to get himself aroused in hopes that something might yet be done.

Dimly, through the fog of his many pains he knew that Jim Tanner had rolled away from him and that the girl was making frantic efforts to determine the extent of their mutual disaster. He grunted, rolled over once, and forced himself to a sitting position. It made his head ache but the action seemed to bring back a certain clarity of thought. He was even conscious of that damp smell of earth and the mustiness of old potatoes which he had noted so illogically when he fell. With just as much lack of good sense he wanted to laugh because Tanner was swearing over and over, "Damn the polecat! Damn the polecat! Damn the polecat!"

"Are you hurt, Tanner?" he asked.

"I ain't sure. Lucky I fell on somethin' soft or I'd be killed."

"Lucky for you. Not so lucky for me. I was the something soft you fell on. For a skinny old rascal you land like something mighty big."

"What about you?" Helen's voice inquired. "Are you hurt?" Her tone helped to bring him back to a proper sense of reality.

"Only my pride, I guess. That Glennister ranny sure put one over on me."

"My fault," Tanner grumbled. "I was a fool to git caught like I did."

"Stop wasting time," the girl cut in sharply. "You'll have a chance to be sorry for yourselves after we've figured out what can be done."

McCall chuckled. "She sounds kinda bossy, Jim," he drawled. "A man hadn't oughta raise up a daughter to be snappy like that. It ain't real lady-like."

"Just another o' my mistakes," the old man complained, adopting McCall's pose of half rueful humor. "What d'ye figure Glennister's plannin' to do now?"

"He'll probably grab a bronc and light a shuck for Latigo Pass. From here on he'll have to stick like a plaster to the rest o' the outlaw crowd."

"And what happens when he tells 'em about you?"

McCall chuckled again. "They'll be sore because he didn't shoot me when he had the chance. Seriously, though, it won't make much difference to me. The gang already know that I'm wise to the rustler trail and orders are out to get me. Glennister's news won't mean anything except that they'll know where to look for me."

There was a shade of irony in the girl's voice as she asked, "Would it be expecting too much if I wanted to know what you're talking about? Who are the rustlers and what else are they doing?"

"Sarcastic as well as bossy, eh?" McCall bantered, trying to relieve the tension a little. "To tell the truth I don't know all the answers yet. All I'm sure of is that there's a pretty well organized gang centering around Marshal Ross Doyle in Latigo Pass. They use the cross canyon in the craglands as a trail for running rustled beef around by a back trail into Latigo. Part of that's guesswork but it's not far wrong. They have another game, too, as I hinted to Glennister, but I don't know what that game is—even though my principal object in coming to Latigo Pass was to get the answer to that very question."

He knew by their silence that they were trying to make the statement fit with his presence here at K-Bar. It didn't seem like any time for long explanations so he changed the subject abruptly. "Now what's the chances of getting out of this hole? I don't even remember this cellar being here so you'll have to offer all the suggestions."

"I ain't so dang sure I want to git out yet," Tanner muttered. "Walt Glennister's still got all the guns, ye know."

A thud of hurrying hooves provided a sufficient reply to that objection. "There he goes," McCall remarked. "If you've got something in mind let's have it. Maybe I can still catch that jigger before he can do more damage."

"Right. Got a match?"

"Sure."

"Move over this way. Toward me. Now strike a light."

McCall followed directions and in the flare of the match was able to see Helen Tanner standing a little to one side while her father fumbled in a little recess where the cellar supports joined the sills of the cabin. At the same time he noted a stub of tallow candle close to the old man's outstretched hand. A second match permitted him to light the candle, and by that time Tanner was dragging an ancient dragoon pistol into view.

"This was why I started to holler when ye talked about puttin' Walt down here," Tanner grunted. "My ace in the hole, so to speak. A man never knows when he might git hard pressed in this country so I cached this old cannon down here fer emergencies." He reached a second time and drew out a buskskin pouch which proved to contain caps and a sealed packet of powder. "I reckon it won't be too much of a trick to shoot the hasp off'n that cellar door."

"Provided our landlord doesn't object to the destruction of his property," the girl suggested, some of the old acid coming back into her voice.

McCall turned to hand her the guttering fragment of candle. "Here. Be some good and stop trying to sound nasty all the time. Hold the light so we can judge where to do the shooting."

She took the candle silently, holding it so that her father could see to load the pistol. McCall went on quietly, using the interval to say some of the things he had been wanting to say. "In case you're still expecting me to be the villain of this piece I might as well tell you that I have every intention of returning to K-Bar if and when I get settled with this outlaw crowd. I think this ranch ought to be a good paying proposition and I propose to have a try at making it pay."

The candle wavered just a little and Tanner stopped suddenly with the wadding halfway down the gun barrel. McCall smiled thinly and added, "I like your plans for the place and I want to have a share in carrying out those plans. Maybe if we work on a partnership basis we'll manage to overcome some of the bad angles that have been cropping up."

Tanner stared in the flickering light. "Then ye ain't plannin' to shove us off'n the place?"

"Of course not. I'll need you—both of you—and I'm hoping you'll need me. We can work out the details after we get rid of this dirty rustling business."

Tanner rammed home the wadding and followed it with a lead ball, his movements suddenly brisk and efficient. "Then let's stop wastin' time with loose gab. We got to git them steers back before the miserable polecats run all the tallow off'n 'em. Hold that light up here, Helen."

One shot did the trick and McCall pushed through the fog of acrid powder smoke to heave the shattered door back. Then he turned to offer a hand to each of the Tanners. In another minute they were out in the sunshine, gasping a little to get the powder fumes out of their nostrils. There was no sign of Glennister on the upper slope but the open corral indicated that he had taken certain precautions before riding away. Every pony was gone.

"We're still in a tight," Tanner grated. "No bronc and no gun exceptin' this old blunderbuss. Got any ideas this time?"

McCall already was scanning the packed earth near the empty corral. "I don't think he took the broncs with him," he called over his shoulder. "Looks like he just turned 'em loose. Got a riata handy?"

Helen had anticipated the request with the first words. Almost before her father could reply she was returning from the ranch house with a coiled rope. McCall took it silently, nodding approval as he caught her eye. Then he started out on the trail of one of the missing broncs; a trail which led toward the wooded slope above the buildings. Back there in the trees he would have a chance of cornering a horse while the prospect of overtaking one on the open range was negligible. Tanner trailed along with him, reloading the old pistol as he walked. Helen spoke only briefly as the men started away. "I'll rustle some grub. If you catch a mount you'll need food before you take the trail."

"Smart girl you've got there, Pop," Larry said, loudly enough for Helen to hear. "When she stops being sharp with the remarks she's quite a help." He glanced back just in time to see her sticking her tongue out at him.

Somehow it seemed like a pleasant gesture, especially when it was done with such a nice smile.

They hurried along into the pine belt on the upper slope, knowing that the loose ponies would not have gone far. Glennister had probably sent them flying with a few licks of a quirt, but the animals would not have run any great distance. With a little luck it might be possible to overtake one promptly. After that it would require patience, skill, and some more luck.

Tanner spotted a bronc first. "One just behind that clump of spruces, Larry," he exclaimed. "Looks like Helen's pet pinto mare. Mebbe I kin sneak up on her; she's purty tame."

"We'll play it the safest way we can," McCall told him. "I'll swing wide and come in from that open space on the right. Then you work in from the left. If you can grab her all right; if you can't she'll have to run toward me because the trees are too thick above and below."

"That's the ticket. Take it easy. I'll give ye a chance to get set before I close in."

McCall nodded and climbed at a wide angle, a little amused at the enthusiasm Tanner was displaying. The amusement was of a slightly grim sort. Tanner was naturally elated to find that he wasn't going to lose his share in K-Bar, but he was letting his happiness make him forget the dangers ahead. Unless the Doyle gang could be eliminated there wouldn't be anyone left to work the ranch. It was going to be a case of kill or be killed now.

As he worked his way through the trees he fashioned a loop such as he had used so many times in shows. Maybe he was going to have some real use for his skill this time.

He had lost sight of the older man so he whistled softly when he was in position along the little ledge which provided an open strip among the trees. Tanner replied with a similar whistle and McCall could hear his wheedling tones as he tried to approach the mare. There was a scurry of hooves and then Tanner swore explosively. "She's runnin', Larry, toward ye. The polecat's got her plumb spooked up."

McCall made certain that no tree branch would foul his cast and as the mare plunged into view he dabbed his loop around her well-groomed neck. One turn around a pine braked her to a gentle halt and he went to her, hand over hand along the restraining lariat. The horse shied just once and then he was on her back, calling to Tanner.

"Ride over this way," the old man shouted in return. "I see another one. We'd better pick him up while we got the chance."

This time it was easy and within five minutes they were riding back toward the ranch house, McCall on Shorty Langan's big sorrel while Tanner rode his daughter's pinto. The old man was chuckling happily. "Looks like this partnership ain't goin' to work out so bad, son. You and me don't make such a half bad team."

"Seems like," McCall agreed, willingly enough. "But we won't crow too soon. There's a dirty job still to be done and I don't like the look of that sky over in the northwest. Some nasty summer squalls come out of that quarter and a hard rain now would make tracking mighty difficult."

"We'll take care o' the trackin', all right," Tanner promised with complete confidence.

"I'll take care of it," McCall corrected, a little amused at the way the old man was letting his excitement run away with him. "You're going to stay right here at K-Bar. You can use the pinto to round up the other broncs—and you'd better get at the chore without delay. We can't make any predictions on the possible storm, but we do know that it won't be long until Glennister will have somebody heading this way. As soon as Doyle finds out what happened he'll send men to square accounts with me. You're in it with me now, you know, so you'll want to be primed against any sort of attack that might come. Play it as safe as possible and I'll try to break the gang from the other end."

"But ye can't swing the job alone. There must be dozens o' them polecats!"

"I've got to try it. Somewhere I'll find help."

Helen insisted upon his eating a hasty meal before riding away and the interval gave the three of them a chance to make sketchy plans. McCall glossed over the difficulties which he knew were before him, not caring to have them worry about his situation, but he made a stern effort to impress them with their own danger. Doyle would have to make an attempt to get rid of them, he warned, so they would have to be ready. It wasn't going to be easy, there being no weapon available but the old pistol, so they would have to make plans accordingly. Perhaps it might even be wise for them to abandon the ranch and head for Mesa until the trouble was over.

That suggestion seemed to bring Tanner's thoughts back to normal. "I got another gun," he announced. "Lemme look and make sure that Walt didn't steal it."

"What about yourself?" Helen asked McCall as her father turned away. "You can't ride after those men unarmed."

"I'm not. When Glennister cut my bronc loose the animal was still saddled, you know. Evidently Walt didn't look in the saddlebags for there was a six-gun there, one that I took from a gent in Latigo Pass last night. It's almost exactly like mine so the ammunition will fit."

Tanner came back, bearing a 45-70 in triumph. "We'll take care of ourselves," he declared. "They won't be sendin' no big gang out here so we'll be able to stick it out 'til ye git back."

Helen's voice had a new note in it as she said simply, "And see that you do get back."

McCall met her eyes and this time neither of them looked away. "I'll promise to make my very best effort," he said soberly. "I'm counting a lot on it."

She did not reply for several moments. Then her words were brief but frank. "So am I."

McCall's thoughts were a curious mixture of bright dreams and grim apprehensions as he sent his mount into the main canyon. Those last few words between Helen Tanner and himself had made him feel that the girl had definitely changed her mind about him. The words had said as much, and her eyes had hinted at something more. It made him conscious of how important the girl had become in his plans for returning to K-Bar. Yesterday he had not been willing to admit the fact, even to himself, but now he let his thoughts run wild. There was going to be a lot of fun in building up K-Bar with a girl like Helen Tanner as a partner. Of course her father was the actual partner, he conceded, but this was no time to foul up a nice dream with technicalities.

It was already too badly fouled with dangers, he knew when he allowed his mind to swing in that direction. And not the least of these at the moment was the storm which had swept up so rapidly over the mountains. The sky was so low that it seemed to rest directly upon the rimrock· and as he sent the pony down the deep canyon which led to the Devil's Cockpit it was like riding through a tunnel. The thunder was rumbling closer all the time and he knew that the Wapitis were in for one of those violent downpours which frequently caused so much trouble in the high country.

Which was all he needed to make the day complete, he thought ruefully. His life was in deadly danger, he had been without sleep for many hours, he had been slugged and thrown down the cellar, he had been fallen upon by Jim Tanner—and now he was going to get soaked. A fine variety of calamities! It would take more than a few bright thoughts about a girl to make a man forget such a collection of woes.

The half humorous complaint brought him around to a consideration of the real problems ahead. He had already thought about the chance of going for help and had discarded the idea as impracticable. There were so few people he could trust, and it was certain that he would have difficulty in getting anyone to believe him. Meanwhile the rustler gang could do its worst. It made the issue squarely a matter for Larry McCall. He had to find some way to outwit the whole crooked gang.

The bravado of the program brought a crooked smile to his lips as he rode southward. Now that Glennister had slipped away to warn his companions there could be but one thing to expect. Instead of McCall chasing rustlers it was going to be rustlers chasing McCall. Which made it seem a little ridiculous for him to be rushing to meet them. A man with half a brain would be making mighty fast tracks in the opposite direction.

He smiled again, grimly amused at his own whimsy. Maybe it didn't make much sense to ride into trouble but there could be no permanent gain in riding away from it. The rustlers would have to be licked now if ever—and McCall knew that he intended to beat them somehow. It was the only way he could return to K-Bar in peace.

He pushed the sorrel as hard as he dared, remembering that the bronc had already done quite a few miles, slackening the pace only when he passed the cut where he had previously come down into the canyon from his exploration of the craglands. From here on he would have to proceed with added caution. There might be any number of enemies just ahead, and he did not propose to gallop headlong into their midst. Not when their intentions were so deadly.

The afternoon had darkened perceptibly as the clouds seemed to drive even lower over the rocky badlands and the lightning flashed with increasing severity. At any moment now the heavens would open up and deluge the crags with one of those downpours which were characteristic of the desert's edge. McCall wanted to beat the storm if possible; he wanted to see the rustler trail before the rain could wash out any sign.

Lightning crashed ominously close as he rode into the niche where he had picketed his horse on that other day. The storm was making the sorrel skittish and it took precious moments before he could get the animal securely tied to a piñon. Then he climbed hastily, anxious to get into position where he could view the Devil's Cockpit before the storm could lash it.

13

It was lighter up there above the canyon but the storm seemed much closer. The wind had subsided into a dead calm while an eerie green light bathed the ugly crags, providing a weird atmosphere which made the mesa seem oppressively unreal. Lightning crashed close behind him as McCall raced for the promontory which divided the two canyons and in the dead silence which followed its resounding roar he could hear a moaning sound which he knew to be wind rushing in to fill this dead spot beneath the threatening clouds.

He had abandoned caution as he ran forward but a single glance told him that the risk had been well taken. The canyons were empty of life. In the ghostly half light the Devil's Cockpit seemed ominously well named, its desolation set off by the storm's gloom until it appeared like a stage setting from some horror play. McCall did not delay with artistic appraisals, however. He went down on his belly at the edge of the cliff, staring hard into the darkening depths in an effort to read the sign which might tell him an important story. It was a pretty hopeless job but he concluded that no substantial force had come into the valley since the passage of the stolen steers. He could not tell whether Walt Glennister had ridden on toward Latigo Pass or into that eastern passage.

One way or another it left him with a hard choice to make. If he took the trail of the rustled beef he would have to take a chance on being trapped. Those Latigo outlaws might close in behind him, boxing him between two halves of the outlaw gang. On the other hand there did not seem to be much point in heading for Latigo. He had met plenty of difficulty in getting away from the town on his last visit and there was no chance that matters would be any easier next time. Probably he was already posted as the killer of Henderson Ott. Doyle would have seen to that.

His decision came quickly as he hurried back to his bronc. He would have to take the rustler trail and run the risks that went with it. No other course offered anything that seemed like a reasonable hope of success.

A gust of wind caught him as he reached the slant which led down into the canyon. It made him grab for a boulder to keep himself from being driven over the edge and then a blast of lightning came, leaving him partly stunned. He shook his head angrily, trying to shake off the effects, and knew that enormous drops of rain were pelting down at him. That tremendous bolt had struck nearby and was bringing the real storm with it. He had to get down the cliff before the rain could make it too slippery.

It was raining hard by the time he slid down the last few feet into the canyon and he raced for the picketed bronc, unlashing his slicker roll with fingers scraped raw by the hasty descent of the cliff.

"Easy, Bo," he soothed the frantic animal. "A little rain won't do you any harm. Stop that doggone prancing and behave yourself like a good Confederate."

He managed to get into the slicker before he was completely soaked but the garment did him little good when the real downpour began. A cold, biting wind swept across the badlands, bringing with it what seemed like a solid wall of black water. It poured into the canyon like a cascade, turning the passage into a swift running stream. At the same time it changed the afternoon into night and made the night a turmoil of driving rain that was broken only by the jagged streaks of vicious lightning.

McCall struggled once to get into the saddle, then he changed his mind and led the pony back into the scant shelter of a rocky overhang. Despite the urgency of the occasion there was no sense in trying to proceed under such conditions. Not only would the pony have to travel in water but there was the grave danger of rock slides caused by the storm. Better to wait and let the worst of the gale blow itself out.

Thunder and lightning seemed to rock the very mountains, and once he was blinded for several moments by a bolt which must have pounded into the crags just above the canyon. Fortunately he had taken the precaution of tying the bronc to a stout pine along the cliff and when the pony started to break in panic there was no chance for him to get away.

The waiting was almost as bad as the physical discomfort. Every minute was giving the enemy that much more time to arrange his strategy and every drop of rain was helping to destroy the trail which he knew he would have to follow. The Wapitis would not have one storm a year like this but it had come at the most inconvenient time.

At the first sign of a break in the weather he climbed into the wet saddle and headed the sorrel into the rapidly diminishing rain. The canyon floor was still under water and washing out badly in the spots where there was anything but solid rock to withstand the cascades which came down from the rimrock. Still he could not be particular. Time was pressing and the day was getting pretty well spent.

The storm broke up with amazing rapidity as a north wind scattered the heavy overcast and by the time he reached the Devil's Cockpit there was a definite opening in the west through which the sun was trying to bore.

He glanced around briefly as he rounded the point of rocks and entered the eastern canyon. The Devil's Cockpit looked as dreary as ever but it was empty. That was consolation enough for the present.

He halted again after passing the canyon's mouth, keeping a tight grip on the nervous pony's reins as he moved in to investigate the niche where Olson's horse had been tethered. It wasn't likely that there would be any sign left after so much rain but it would not take many minutes for a quick look and he had a hunch that the place might be a regular stop for the rustler gang.

Water was still pouring down through the break in the cliff wall and he saw at once that the storm had ripped through here with considerable fury. One rock slide hinted that a bolt of lightning might have crashed into the rim just above the cranny, but mostly the place showed water damage. Tree roots were washed bare in many spots and the whole opening had been swept clean of years' accumulation of soil.

He was about to turn away when he caught sight of a regular object which did not fit in with the eccentric outlines of rocks and shale. It was a substantial looking box wedged behind a couple of small boulders. He tied the sorrel to a pine which still seemed to be firmly rooted and stooped to examine his find. The box was rough made but sturdy. Its hasp came loose easily enough and he opened it to find a sodden bit of paper and the stub of a pencil inside. He scanned the paper without venturing to touch it, fearful that it would fall apart in his fingers. On it someone had made a series of notations in firm but crude characters.

$$14 \quad \wedge$$
$$6 \quad \boxdot$$
$$10 \quad \circ\!\!-$$
$$7 \quad W$$

A little below these another line had been added in a different hand.

$$11 \quad \mathsf{K}$$

At the very bottom of the paper, in still different characters had been scrawled:

Mc in K seller. W

McCall considered the exhibit carefully before making a move. This box was evidently one of those outlaw post offices which were so common in hideout country. Located here at the crossing of the canyons it offered a convenient means of communication between the various divisions of the outlaw crowd. In this case the actual rustlers had left an itemized account of their most recent raid, informing some expected rider from Latigo Pass that they were moving down the canyon with a stolen herd made up of fourteen head from Rafter, six from Box-Dot, ten from Frying Pan, and seven from the Flying W. After that they had added the eleven from K-Bar.

That information had been left by the riders of the early morning, but then Walt Glennister had come along to add his hasty notice. Evidently he must have ridden into the eastern canyon for his message must have been directed toward someone expected out from Latigo Pass. After that had come the cloudburst, the rain washing away the protective layer of sand which probably had been used to cover the box.

For a moment McCall considered leaving the message intact, hoping that it might prove useful as evidence, but then he changed his mind and transferred the wet paper carefully to a shirt pocket. He didn't want to direct any kind of an attack at the Tanners if he could avoid it, and Walt Glennister's message about McCall being in the K-Bar cellar would certainly have such an effect. Better to take it along and gamble that Glennister would not be able to deliver his message elsewhere.

The sorrel was still showing the effects of the storm scare and as McCall led him out into the open canyon he pranced away, swinging his hind quarters in a circle as he tried to dodge the rider. McCall spoke soothingly as he pulled the bronc down, but the pony bucked again as McCall lifted a foot toward the stirrup.

It put him hopelessly off balance just as three men rode into the canyon behind him. Their guns were in their fists and he saw instantly that resistance was hopeless. He caught his balance and obeyed the shouted order to raise his hands.

Almost as quickly he realized that these men were not members of the rustler outfit, so far as he knew. He had not seen any of them in Latigo Pass and he did not believe they were riders who had been on the trail this morning. Two were ordinary looking waddies in muddy, battered range outfits while the third was a stout, red-faced man of fifty whose sagging wet vest bore a somewhat dented star. Stallcup's story came back to McCall and he decided that this must be Sheriff Brodheiser, if that was the name. Maybe this wasn't going to turn out to be such a disaster after all.

The trio closed in warily, guns tense. Suddenly the younger of the two deputies barked an excited comment. "Looks like we picked him up first crack outa the box, Sheriff. He fits the description all right."

"Hold it a bit," McCall broke in. "If you're Sheriff Brodheiser, mister, you'd better give me a chance to tell you a couple o' things."

The round red face was expressionless under the sodden black hat. "Brodheiser's the name," he snapped. "And we're goin' to give yuh plenty o' time to talk. Later. Pick up his gun, Curt!"

The young deputy dismounted and moved in smartly to snake the forty-five out of McCall's holster. Not content with that he reached out to slap the wet garments which clung to the redhead until every line of his lean body was apparent. "No knife, Sheriff," he reported.

"Take a look at his bedroll and saddlebags."

"I don't know what you're looking for, Sheriff," McCall interrupted, "but you're wasting a lot of valuable time here. I'm Larry McCall and if you've talked to Gordon Stallcup in Latigo Pass you must know something of what I'm doing out here. There's a gang of rustlers working this country and I've . . ."

"No knife, Sheriff," the deputy broke in calmly.

"We won't need it, Curt," the red-faced man said with a satisfied smile. "He's being right nice to us. Admits he's McCall. I reckon that's enough."

"Why shouldn't I?" Larry demanded. "What's going on here?"

Brodheiser smiled again. "Maybe he'll even clean up the whole case for us while he's in a good mood. How about it, McCall? Going to confess that you knifed that Jones hombre and shot Henderson Ott?"

"You're crazy! I didn't . . ."

"Then we ain't goin' to be so lucky, after all," the sheriff complained. "Well, a man can't expect too much. Climb on yore bronc and we'll play our little games with yo' when we're back in Latigo. My poor old tail is gettin' plumb tired o' settin' in a wet saddle. Watch him, Dan, while Curt climbs back on his hoss."

McCall tried again, desperately. "You've got to listen to me, Sheriff. I didn't kill anybody—in Latigo Pass or anywhere else. The rustler outfit is using their own killing job to crowd me. They know I'm onto their game and they're trying to put me in the bad with you."

"Hit leather!" the stout man barked, his bland good humor disappearing suddenly. "Doyle warned me that you'd likely try to smoke up the case with outlaw talk. And Stallcup wasn't any too sure of you, now that I think about it."

"All right. Keep an eye on me—but don't let this gang get away with it. Send a man down this canyon to see what happened to the gang. Or let me lead the way and you can go along to watch me. I'm telling you that a herd of rustled beef was driven through here at daylight this morning."

"It looks like it, don't it?" Brodheiser was elaborately sarcastic as he stared around him. "Just the country for a cattle trail."

"But I tell you this is a cattle trail for rustled beef. If that storm hadn't come along you could see plenty of sign to prove what I'm telling you."

Brodheiser laughed grimly. "That ain't such a good

yarn to tell, son. A smart fella like yo're supposed to be oughta do better than that. Get on that bronc!"

McCall mounted, raging inwardly at the way fate was conspiring with Sheriff Brodheiser's stupidity to ruin everything. The stout man clucked genially, going back to his pose of easy good humor. "Let's ride, boys. I ain't what yo' might call real happy when I'm so wet."

"Fine lawman!" McCall snapped. "Anything to get dry clothes. What difference does it make if a gang of outlaws go free?"

Brodheiser motioned for the deputies to close in on either side of the prisoner. His eyes had narrowed a little at McCall's criticism, but he managed to maintain his even tones as he murmured, "Always another day for hunting rustlers even if they are mostly imaginary ones. Fer today I reckon it's enough to bring in a killer."

The deputies followed his signaled instructions and the quartet moved out into the Devil's Cockpit. It took a minute or two before McCall could get the anger and desperation out of his voice, but finally he managed to ask, "Would you mind telling me just what the charge is against me, Sheriff? Maybe we can straighten this mess out before we get into it too deep."

"Yo're a right cool hand," the stout man observed blandly. "No harm in talkin'. It'll help to pass the time while we shove on back to Latigo Pass, and mebbe keep me from thinkin' about how uncomfortable a pair o' wet pants can get. Yo're accused o' stickin' a knife into a feller name of Jones. Little mousy lookin' critter, in case the name don't mean anything to yo'. It seems like yo' done it because he was runnin' yo' down fer the shootin' of Henderson Ott."

"I didn't do any part of it, of course," McCall stated, trying to acquire some of the sheriff's annoying calmness. "If I'm supposed to have killed Jones because he was after me for the Ott killing, why am I supposed to have killed Ott?"

"Nobody was just shore about that part but it seems like yo' had a fracas with Ott the other night. Somethin' about a lady, I believe. That part ain't so important, though, because we got a first class witness to the Jones killin'. United States Deputy Marshal Akers seen yo' pull the job, but he was just too slow to catch up with yo'. Nobody has figured out yet how yo' managed to slip outa town but that ain't important either."

"He's ridin' a Langan bronc," the older deputy cut in. "Maybe that oughta tell us somethin'."

It told McCall something but it also left him at a loss for words. Apparently the Langan account about being held up by a stranger had not been told to Sheriff Brodheiser. Why not? Had Shorty held it back or had Doyle suppressed it? One way or another the evidence was now pointing to Langan as an accomplice and McCall could not do any explaining until he knew just what sort of crooked charge had been cooked up against him. Anything he might say now could easily prove to be the wrong thing.

The sun was getting pretty low at the west end of the pass when they emerged upon the long down grade into Latigo Pass, and by that time McCall had decided that he would have to take a chance. He would have to tell his entire story and hope that Brodheiser would believe at least a part of it. If he could put even a little doubt in the lawman's mind it might help.

"Look, Sheriff," he said as quietly as he could manage. "I don't know what this United States marshal thinks he saw, but he's way off the track if he claims he saw me kill anybody. I do know that it smells plenty bad when everything in Latigo is considered. Marshal Ross Doyle is the biggest crook in town and I'm layin' odds that he's the jigger framed this thing on me."

"Take it easy," the fat man advised, still lazily good-natured. "Yo'll have plenty o' chance to gab when we get to Latigo. Yo'll be able to talk all yo' want through the bars o' Doyle's nice cool jail."

Doyle's jail! The words were ominous. The Latigo crowd had rigged up a crooked charge and were letting the sheriff do the dirty work for them. McCall had a hunch that Brodheiser was honest in his stupidity, but it didn't help any. Once the prisoner was behind bars it would only be a question of time until Doyle and his henchmen would promote some kind of a rioting lynch mob. It was certain that they would not risk having McCall talk in a public trial.

The presence of a United States Marshal in Latigo offered a ray of hope, but it wasn't a very bright one. Sheriff Brodheiser said the federal man was the star witness in the case against McCall. That could mean any one of several things—none of them good. The marshal had been fooled by Doyle's crowd or he was working with them. Then another possibility came to McCall's mind and he had a feeling that he was groping very close to a true explanation. Not that it helped much. He was about be to a prisoner in the enemy's jail.

14

They kept up a pretty fair pace down the grade to Latigo Pass, a fact which made conversation a little difficult. McCall tried to argue at every opportunity but he didn't seem to get anywhere with it. His captors listened to him when he told the story of the cross canyon and the rustler organization but they made it clear that they were being entertained rather than informed. Evidently they had been primed to expect some rather fantastic yarns from him, and he could only suppose that somebody had helped Ross Doyle to plant the ideas in their minds. He could not quite believe that

Doyle had been clever enough to do it, but someone had certainly cooked up a smart plot to hang a murder charge on him, working in enough details to make the real truth sound like something from the imagination.

On the credit side McCall learned a few things from the sheriff and his deputies. They were willing to talk, even though they did so with an air of banter, evidently believing that he already knew too much about the things they were telling him. That fellow Jones, for example. He had not been well known in Latigo Pass. Marshal Doyle believed that he might have been a fugitive who had come to hide out in Latigo Pass. Jones had been very quiet, however, and there had been no trouble connected with his presence in town.

The deputies talked a little more interestedly on the subject of United States Marshal Akers. McCall gathered that the man was a deputy marshal, but Brodheiser's men gave him the larger title in discussing him. The federal man's evidence had been definite and damning so far as McCall was concerned. He stated that he saw McCall entering a dark lane just west of the Silver Strike Hotel. Seconds later Jones ran into the same alley as though in pursuit of McCall. Akers followed and was able to see a clear silhouette of a brief struggle at the far end of the alley. The taller man, McCall, had stabbed the smaller one. He ran forward but Jones was already dead and McCall had disappeared completely.

It had made an awkward choice for the federal man, so the story went. He had not wanted to advertise his presence in Latigo Pass but he knew that he could not suppress such evidence. It was not until he reported to Marshal Ross Doyle that he discovered that McCall was already wanted on suspicion of having shot a land agent named Henderson Ott.

Darkness had fallen across the barren flats of the pass when the little cavalcade passed the first adobes of the

132

north side. By that time the deputies had tightened their guard over the prisoner, one of them riding behind with drawn gun while the other kept a rope on McCall's bronc. They were not taking any chances on a sudden break from the man who had built himself a quick reputation for fast moves.

McCall smiled wryly at the elaborate precautions. His eyes were burning from loss of sleep, his whole body ached from fatigue and from the bumps he had taken in the potato cellar, and his mind had reached a point of weariness where it seemed physically impossible to think. These deputies might have saved themselves a lot of nervousness if they had only realized how completely spent their prisoner was.

Even when they passed Langan's Lone Star Livery McCall found it hard to make himself think. Something in the back of his tired mind kept beating for recognition but he could not quite get around to paying attention. In a dull way he recalled that previous evening when Doyle's men had searched for him and he had outwitted them. Only last night, it must have been; looking back it seemed like a year ago. Ott had already been murdered, he remembered. When had Jones got it?

It was something of a surprise to him to hear the steadiness of his own words as he asked, "When did you say this stabbing business took place?"

One of the deputies grunted. "A fine question, mister, comin' from yo'. Just in case it mighta slipped yore mind I'll tell yo' it was jest about midnight. A couple o' minutes one way or another. Remember now?"

"Thanks," McCall said quietly. "I remember well enough that I was back in the mountains by midnight. I've been trying to guess whether this was a dirty job or a case of mistaken identity. Now I know. No federal marshal or anybody else saw me in Latigo at midnight last night; I simply was not here."

"Dam' shame yo' can't prove it."

133

McCall ignored the patent sarcasm in the comment. "Ain't it though?" he agreed.

That amount of conversation seemed to be the limit for his flagging energies. He tried to think about United States Deputy Marshal Akers but his mind would not stick to the subject. It was all he could do to remain in the saddle, and he was half asleep when the little cavalcade halted in front of the adobe calaboose which he had noticed on the first night in Latigo. He knew that he was being guarded closely as they hustled him behind iron gratings but there was only a dull feeling of surprise that Ross Doyle should not appear on the scene. After that he didn't remember anything until he awoke to find the sun streaming through a tiny window cut high in the wall.

He sat up quickly, realizing that a new day was well into its morning. Physically he felt a little better. There were still plenty of aches in his mistreated bones and muscles but the deadly weariness was gone and his mind was clear. Too clear for comfort, perhaps. Even as he opened his eyes he had been unhappily aware of the peril of his position.

Most of the grim facts ran promptly through his mind as he perched himself on the edge of the bare bunk, but the one item which loomed largest in his thoughts was the part about a federal officer giving testimony against him. That might be the tip-off on the whole show. Certainly no one, officer or not, had seen him going into a lane with anyone at midnight on the night in question. At that hour he had been urging the sorrel to the task of climbing the Wapiti slope in the darkness. If the evidence was false then it seemed likely that the officer might be a fake also. But why had the gang seen fit to call their crooked witness a federal man? That ought to mean something.

A noise outside the calaboose caught his attention and he watched the door open to admit the young deputy who had ridden with Sheriff Brodheiser. The man was carrying a decently laden tray of food and there was a wariness in his eyes which did not seem to contain any particular enmity. Still he took due precautions with his prisoner, evidently having been warned about giving McCall any kind of escape opportunity.

He placed the tray on the floor of the cell and backed out quickly, locking the iron door behind him. "Better eat hearty, McCall," he said, grinning a little. "Yo've already missed breakfast by sleepin' so long and I dunno when yo'll git fed again."

"This'll hold me," McCall told him. "Particularly when you're the one that brings it. Now I know Doyle hasn't managed to take over yet."

"Still giving me that song and dance about Doyle, are yuh?" the deputy commented, his gray eyes narrowing in a look which gave McCall a tinge of hope. Somehow the man seemed to be a little dubious about something. Maybe he had begun to suspect the motives of Latigo's lawman.

"Why not?" McCall countered, attacking the breakfast. "I was telling you men the truth last night. Doyle is a thief—and probably a killer. He knows I've got the goods on him and he's out to shut me up. While the sheriff's office is handling the business I can hope for a square deal; if Doyle takes charge I'm a dead duck!"

The deputy looked around nervously. "Got any way to prove you're workin' for Apache?" he asked.

"Nothing but the card I showed Stallcup. In my business a man doesn't carry stuff like birth certificates and his eighth grade diploma. Generally he can't afford to have 'em found on him."

"Then you can't prove who you are?"

"Sure I can. At least one person in Latigo Pass knows that I'm Larry McCall. A wire to Apache's main office will verify my business here."

"But it won't show that you didn't kill them two jaspers." The deputy stated it as a fact which he somehow deplored, and McCall began to have hopes that the questioning might indicate a change of heart on the part of Sheriff Brodheiser.

"Have you checked on this federal man?" he asked. "I think he's a ringer."

The deputy shook his head. "We talked about it but the sheriff figured it wasn't much use. Government men have to take their chances like you claim you do. Mostly they don't have papers to show and their headquarters won't own 'em unless they feel like it. Akers had a badge and a card but he told us he didn't think his home office would tell us anything about him. That's because of the kind of job he's on."

"So nobody tried?"

"Nope."

"What does Akers look like?"

"He's a tall, rawboned galoot with a bald head. Why?"

"I was wondering. I still think he's a fake. If you want to do the sheriff a favor you'll persuade him to ask the federal authorities for a description of this man Akers. And I'll give you odds that it won't fit this jasper you described."

The young fellow seemed impressed. "I'd talk to him about it," he muttered, "only he ain't in town now."

"No. Why not?"

"He got a call about an hour ago. Somebody shot up a few ore wagons out at the mine last night. There was a train of wagons ready to pull out at dawn and somebody raided the depot. We didn't get no more details but Brodheiser took Dan with him and hustled out to have a look-see. He won't be back 'til tomorrow so I'm in charge here."

"Which means you're in a nasty spot," McCall told him quietly. "Brodheiser gets tolled out of town so Doyle can find a way to keep me from having my say

136

in any kind of a court. It means that they've got to get rid of you next. Better keep your eyes skinned for trouble."

The man seemed impressed. "Mebbe you ain't as far outa the way as we figgered," he conceded dubiously. "Somehow I don't like the looks o' things in this town."

"Then ask Gordon Stallcup to wire Apache headquarters about me. Get him to ask for instructions and to have the main office request a check on Akers. But don't depend on Stallcup if you find yourself in a tight place. He's honest, I reckon, but if there's trouble you'd better find some way to get Shorty Langan handy for a helper.'"

"We'll see," the deputy retorted uncomfortably. He seemed to be torn between two conflicting interests. Apparently he had seen something in Latigo Pass which made him distrust the motives of Marshal Ross Doyle, but still he had a duty to perform. He was even a little embarrassed because he had let himself converse so freely with a prisoner. To McCall it offered a ray of hope. The young fellow might be a hesitant sort but he was showing signs of honesty. That was something.

The afternoon dragged by in ominous silence. No one came into the jail even to pick up the food tray, and McCall found plenty of time to ponder over the many angles of his awkward predicament. Almost for the first time he had an inkling of the real truth behind the seemingly aimless pattern of small scale rustling. There was plenty still to be explained but he thought he knew most of the answers—now that he was in no position to use the knowledge.

For the present he knew that his only hope lay in that worried young deputy with the gray eyes. The man must know a part of the true story or he would not have listened so much this morning. He did not have the makings of a particularly stout ally, but he would be better than none. Certainly some kind of help

137

would have to appear if disaster were to be averted. It was a dead cinch that Doyle could not afford to have McCall brought before a public hearing, which meant that an attempt would certainly be made to silence the prisoner.

Twice during the long afternoon McCall slept, the old weariness and the dead heat of the jail serving to overcome his worries. When he awoke after the second nap he knew that the sun was getting pretty low in the west. Just as quickly he realized that his doze had been interrupted by the sound of footsteps beyond the door of the calaboose. Two sets of footsteps this time.

A flash of apprehension swept over him but it was the young deputy who stepped into the darkened interior, his thin features set in a perplexed frown. Behind him came the man McCall had seen that first evening in Latigo, the man who had helped Ross Doyle to haul away the unconscious form of Jake Zellers from the alley. Wells, the town marshal had named him. A comparative stranger to Latigo Pass, the gossips had said. Seeing him for the first time in partial daylight McCall saw that he was not a particularly big man but a sturdy one. He was smooth-shaven, black-eyed and with a tinge of gray in his dark hair. There was no expression in either the dark eyes or the hard face. One of Doyle's hired guns, probably.

The young deputy caught McCall's appraising glance and shook his head. Then he spoke with an effort at crispness, addressing the taciturn man who had followed him into the jail.

"Here's what I wouldn't say outside, Wells. This is the prisoner. And I want to see him here when I get back. Until further notice he's in your charge. Make sure that nothing happens to him!"

"Right." Wells did not seem particularly concerned. "Any reason why I had to come in here for that speech?"

The deputy seemed bothered by the other man's casual distinterest. Wells seemed so sure of himself—and the deputy so obviously was not. "Plenty good reason," he snapped. "I don't like the looks of this setup at all. Sheriff Brodheiser's tryin' to run this country honest, and that means a fair trial for any man he arrests. We don't want nobody haulin' prisoners outa jail for no lynchin' bees!"

Wells was still unmoved. "I reckon I can understand that," he agreed, no trace of interest in his voice.

His calmness seemed to infuriate the nervous deputy. "Make sure yo' remember it," he barked. "If this man ain't here when I git back I'm personally goin' to raise plenty of hell about it."

"Suits me. Just keep in mind that I didn't ask for this jailer job."

The younger man swung to stare through the bars at McCall. "I'm tellin' yo' just how it is, mister. And I'm goin' to tell a few other folks before I head outa town. That's the best I can do, I reckon."

McCall knew a quick sense of dread. "You're leaving Latigo?"

"Yep. Got orders. About fifteen minutes ago a note came in from the sheriff down at the mines. It's an honest note, all right; I know his style o' scribblin'. He wants me to start for the mines right away, leavin' yo' under guard of local authorities."

"Lucky for you," McCall said, trying to keep the anger out of his tone. "Now they won't have to shoot you to get at me."

The younger man squirmed uneasily. "I reckon I know how yo' feel. If there was any doubt about the note I'd figure it was the same kind of a skin game yo' said they'd try. Mebbe it's still part of the rawhidin' idea, but I got to obey orders."

"Plumb touchin' ain't it?" Wells drawled, apparently amused at the deputy's agitation.

The young lawman ignored him, speaking swiftly to McCall. "All I can do is to make sure that folks know what to look for—and to let the crooks know that any move they make will be spotted for what it is."

"Stop beatin' around the bush," Wells cut in. "What's on yore chest?"

"This. I think there's a dirty frameup against this man here. I think somebody wants to get rid of him before he has a chance to sound off in public. Maybe this note from the sheriff is a part of a scheme to get at him. That's why I'm warnin' yo' that if anything happens to him I'll see that this town gits turned inside out. Yo' better find yorself about a dozen good citizens, if yo've got any here, and put a guard around the buildin'. Tell 'em to shoot anybody that makes a move toward the place. I'll take the responsibility."

McCall wished that the deputy's determination could be as fierce as his excited words. In that case he might ignore the sheriff's note and stick around.

Wells shrugged. "Kinda excited, ain't yo'? When do I take over?"

"Make it in twenty minutes. That'll give me time to get ready and give yo' time to bring in some grub for the prisoner. And yo' might haul them dishes back to the Silver Strike. That's where the other meal came from so they might as well keep on handlin' the job."

"Fine," McCall commented ironically. "Now I can have a piece of my own stolen beef before I get shot for knowing too much about it."

The deputy stopped his nervous pacing long enough to unlock the cell door so Wells could come in and pick up the dirty dishes. No one spoke again until after Wells had gone out. Then the deputy came close to the barred door and stared worriedly at his prisoner. "I still don't like this thing, McCall, but I figure I got to obey orders. Yo'll be all right, maybe, if these hombres know that folks are on the lookout for dirty tactics."

"I'd feel better riding with you," McCall suggested. "The note didn't say that you couldn't bring the prisoner along, did it?"

"Yes, it did. Brodheiser specially mentioned that I was to turn yo' over to Doyle. The marshal ain't in town and neither is any of his deputies so I picked this Wells jasper. Folks seemed to figure that he would answer to Doyle and I wanted to put somebody like that in a place where they'd have to take the responsibility. I reckon it's the best I can do for yo'."

"I can't argue. Anyway, it'll be a great consolation for my departed spirit to know that some of Doyle's boys will have some explaining to do."

The bitterness in the words was not entirely lost upon the deputy. "Sorry," he said shortly. "I'm not what yo'd call real happy about this, yo' know, but mebbe we're both makin' it sound worse than it is. I'm countin' kinda big on Doyle bein' afraid to make a move when he finds out I've spread the word about such bein' the prospects."

"Then you're counting too much on his stupidity," McCall retorted. "Doyle's a smart hombre. He knows where his best chances lie and it's a cinch he'll see the point to this one. If he lets his gang come in here and act like a lynch mob he'll have some explainin' to do. All right, he'll do it. Don't think he won't find some kind of an out, some way to blame it all on men who can afford to get out of sight for a while. On the other hand, if he lets me alone he knows what he's in for. I'll tell my story and then he won't have any chance to make an explanation hold up. He's got to get rid of me and he knows it. One way he's got a chance and the other way he doesn't have any. Figure it out for yourself."

The deputy had been backing toward the door as McCall snapped out the words. It was clear enough that he understood the significance of the logic but it was equally clear that he had made up his mind to leave.

"Sorry," he repeated awkwardly. "I got to take the chance."

Then the door slammed behind him and McCall was left alone to the realization that this could be almost the end of the trail.

15

The deputy did not return, but Wells came back swearing under his breath as he stumbled into the darkened jail. McCall could hear the clatter of dishes as the man put his burden down on the floor, then light sprang up as Wells struck a match and set it to the lantern which hung in the narrow corridor. Then the outside door opened again to admit a second man and McCall found himself staring into the baleful green eyes of Jake Zellers. A peculiar grunt came from Wells but his expression was blank as ever when McCall looked at him.

No one said a word. In a tight silence Wells picked up the tray and brought it to the cell, jerking his head in a warning for McCall to stay back as he unlocked the door. Zellers moved a couple of steps, his hand on his gun as though to back the jailer in the event of trouble. McCall ignored his old antagonist and looked interestedly at the meal.

"Nice-looking steak," he observed blandly. "Too bad you couldn't do as well with the deputy sheriff's orders about getting a few honest citizens as guards. It's a cinch Jake Zellers won't fit the requirements."

Zellers rumbled angrily, still keeping a fist on the gun butt. "That's it, Blabbermouth. Get the smart talk outa yer system while ye've still got breath." He laughed harshly and added, "Ain't it too bad that we was so busy pickin' up a good meal fer the pris'ner that we plumb forgot to git him any nice honest guards? Now somethin's liable to happen."

McCall started to reach for the food but a faint shake of the head from Wells caused him to hold back. Somehow he had imagined that the jailer had been about to speak to him when Zellers had come in. Now the man was giving him some sort of warning. It was as enigmatic as it was unexpected, but McCall was in no position to ignore any kind of a hint. He had to play along with any hunch that might offer a faint hope.

Trying to kill time while he searched for an answer he grinned aggravatingly at Zellers. "Somethin' will likely happen, eh?" he commented, mimicking Jake's tone. "It beats all how things manage to happen when you and I get together. I just wish all my enemies were as easy as you, Jake."

The grimy hand closed a little more firmly over the gun butt and Wells stepped hastily in front of the angry man. "Don't let him rile you, Jake," he soothed. "Your turn's comin' later. Keep your head."

"The hell with it. I'll kill him now. Then nobody will have to figure out any fancy answers."

"No." The jailer's tone was firm. "Doyle's got this all planned. Better stick to your orders. Come on outside and let him alone."

"Yeah," McCall chimed in, still wondering. "You spoil my appetite, Zellers. Even in a jail you're no ornament."

Wells practically pushed the angry gunman out into the night, leaving McCall to chuckle a little grimly at his own ill-timed humor. Somehow he had an idea that Wells was trying to help him; he'd have to be careful that he didn't do anything to ruin whatever plan might be afoot.

A part of the answer came promptly enough, even though it left him with a whole grist of new questions to think about. Under his coffee cup he found a bit of folded paper. On the paper were the words, "Don't try to escape. Ambush." The writing was definitely feminine and he remembered seeing letters like that before, probably on the register at the Silver Strike.

The meaning seemed clear enough. Daisy was warning him that Doyle's plan was the old one of giving a prisoner a chance to break jail so that he might be shot down by waiting guards. But Wells had known about the message, judging by the way he had acted. What did that mean?

Again there was a fairly obvious answer. Wells was partly in the confidence of the Doyle gang, but not entirely. Zellers was watching him. That would account for the failure to secure citizen guards. What the connection might be between Wells and Daisy was a matter for only wild guessing.

He thought it over carefully as he ate, considering the chance that the whole thing might be some kind of elaborate double-cross. That was one of the worst features of the whole show; he did not know whom to trust. Maybe Wells was all right and maybe he was simply playing a deep game. Maybe this note was a fake, designed to trap him into doing whatever the gang wanted him to do. Nor was it helpful to realize that when the time came for a decision he would probably have to take whatever risk appeared.

Nearly two hours passed before the door opened again. This time the visitor was Jake Zellers and he was alone. The squatty man seemed to have shed his anger but it had been replaced by a malevolent cockiness that was even more threatening. Jake seemed pretty well pleased with himself and McCall knew that it could only mean a ripening of the outlaw plans.

"Time to haul the dishes away, chum," Zellers announced. "Got to have everything cleaned up spick and span in case we need this cell for another customer."

144

"Meaning that you're expecting to lose me?"

"Permanent." The Zellers grin was ominously genial. "Things happen awful sudden around Latigo Pass—and they couldn't happen to a better hombre."

"Thanks. Where's Wells?"

Zellers made a brisk show of drawing his gun as he moved forward to unlock the cell door. There was nothing playful, however, about the way he kept his gun trained on McCall's middle while he slipped inside to pick up the supper tray. "Pore Wells," he sighed, almost comic in his efforts to put on an exaggerated frown. "Somebody musta kidnapped him. Which mebbe wasn't so bad for Wells. He was the jasper what was supposed to be responsible fer yuhr carcass, so he needed a good alibi fer what's likely to happen any time now."

"Nice of you to take care of him."

"Ain't it though? Folks might git to askin' questions when this here *juzcado* gits raided but they won't be able to blame Wells when they find out he's been hawg-tied and helpless all night."

He had been backing out as he talked, juggling the dishes with one hand while he kept the gun lined on McCall. It wasn't difficult for him to look pretty clumsy in the business of locking the cell door but McCall felt that the clumsiness was partly assumed. Zellers must have known perfectly well that the door was not latched when he turned the key in the lock.

Larry restrained the urge to gamble on an immediate attack. Instead he matched the heavy humor with an irony of his own. "And I suppose you're playing waiter so as to display your own lily-white innocence? You'll be over at the hotel with people ready to vouch for you when the attack comes."

"Sometimes," Jake said sourly, "I think it's almost a shame to kill yuh. Yuh're sech a smart pup. G'bye now; mebbe yuh won't be so noisy the next time I look at yuhr ugly phiz."

145

"Don't take any bets on it."

Zellers grinned. McCall thought he understood what was passing through the gunman's mind. Jake had it all figured out that the prisoner was primed and ready to take quick advantage of that loose door, ready to make a break before the advertised raid could take place. Which was exactly what was wanted.

"Sweet dreams," Jake said and went out.

Now the stage is set, McCall told himself. But for what? He considered the story that the outlaws would be able to tell in the morning. It wasn't such a bad one for their purposes. Guards had been posted according to the deputy sheriff's order. In spite of their vigilance somebody had sneaked in and caught Wells foul. Meanwhile Zellers had been over at the Silver Strike, returning dishes. At that point the prisoner had made a break with the aid of his mysterious helpers and in the excitement had been shot down, his confederates escaping. What could be neater? No one could prove anything different and there would be no one to blame but the dead prisoner.

He could hear the crunch of Jake's departing footsteps and once the sound faltered as though the man had paused to pass a parting comment to one of the waiting gunmen. The trap was set and ready to be sprung, but McCall knew that he could not afford to be idle. If he did not make some pretense of escape the outlaws would simply alter their plans and come in to get him. It would not be too difficult for them to haul him outside for the actual killing. No one would be able to tell the difference afterward.

He thought briefly about stirring up a loud row in hopes of attracting attention from the town but abandoned the idea at once. The jail was not close enough to the main part of the village for the risk to be a good one. It probably would accomplish no purpose except to spur the ambushers on to speedier action.

Then he moved, gambling that the waiting killers were in no position to strike until he had cleared the building. One bound put him in the cell corridor and a second later he had extinguished the lantern. Darkness made him feel a little more secure but he traded his energy for caution as he moved toward the outer door. If the guards were expecting him to break right out into the open as a fair target they were going to get fooled.

He opened the door silently, holding it ajar without exposing himself to possible raking shots. The night was silent except for the distant drone of voices along the streets but he did not deceive himself. Somewhere out there men were waiting for him to step into view. He could only hope that his present course of action would goad them into making some move which would give him the chance he needed so sorely.

Minutes went by and he began to wonder whether this waiting game might not be more nerve-racking for him than for those silent watchers. Then he heard the stealthy rustle of a movement in the darkness behind the adjoining building. The sound was repeated and then a warning hiss came to his ears. Almost at the same instant there was a startled grunt and the sound of a dull but heavy blow.

McCall strained his eyes trying to see into the blackness of the night but there was nothing visible, only a continued sound of a body moving cautiously. His own helplessness was more apparent than ever as he knew a hope that somewhere out there help might be developing. On sudden impulse he turned away from the door and caught up the hot lantern, holding it ready as he slid back to his post. Even a lantern might do duty in a pinch.

Once more there was an interval of flat silence and McCall began to feel discouraged again. For a moment he had hoped that some sort of help had arrived but now he decided that he had heard simply the clumsy stumbling of one of the waiting gunman. He realized that he had been gripping the lantern's handle until the wire was cutting into the flesh of his wet fingers so he shifted it to the other hand, striving for a measure of self-control even as he kept himself taut and ready. Sooner or later something would have to break. Those gunnies wouldn't wait all night. They had to get him while the prearranged alibis were in force.

He wondered about those alibis. What arrangements had been made to keep Doyle in the clear? And where had the giant marshal been for the past twenty-four hours? How had he contrived to get Brodheiser to send that note? And how had Daisy gotten wind of the plot?

There was no time to do more than let the questions run through his mind. Another sound came to break the tension, the sound of a man moving restlessly at the side of the jail itself. On the heels of the movement came a whispered, "Manuel! What's up?"

The reply sounded from the dark area where those earlier noises had originated. It was only the single word, "Quiet," but to McCall's ear it did not sound like the voice of the tall Mexican. Maybe his first hope had been a good one.

Evidently the questioner had not noticed the difference for he spoke again, dropping all pretense of secrecy this time. "No use waitin', Manuel. The polecat's bein' cagey. We gotta yank him outa there. Come on."

McCall poised himself for a desperation battle. He could hear a quick movement at the corner of the jailhouse and a corresponding shuffle from the more distant shadow. Then with a nerve-shattering suddenness a gun boomed. He could see the orange flame across the yard and knew that it had not been aimed at him.

It could mean but one thing and he swung into action even as two more shots shattered the night. Throwing the door wide open he sprang into the yard, ready to give aid to the unknown who had blasted his way into the middle of the ambush. Even as he jumped he heard Shorty Langan's triumphant yelp.

"I got him, Larry. He was down before I put that last shot into him. This way quick!"

He could see the diminutive form of the stableman emerging from the shadow, but he did not halt until he was crouching over the inert form of the man Shorty had cut down. "With you in a jiffy," he called. Then he was unbuckling the dead man's gun belt and pawing around on the ground for the fallen gun.

"No time for that," Shorty urged, close beside him now. "We're goin' to have plenty hornets in our ears in about half a minute. Let's git outa here."

"This won't take long. Got to throw 'em off the trail if we can. Here. Hold this catridge belt for me." He picked up the dead man's gun and stuck it in the waistband of his levis, aware that men were shouting in the street. There wasn't going to be much of a margin of safety here.

Shorty protested again as McCall grabbed the dead man by one arm and dragged him to the door of the calaboose. "Let him lay, Larry," the little man squeaked. "He's dead and we got to be makin' tracks."

"He's dead all right," McCall grunted. "That's why this won't hurt him any." He heaved the corpse into the building and picked up the discarded lantern, smashing it against the doorway. Then he lighted a match and touched it deliberately to the widening pool of oil.

"That'll give them something to think about," he muttered. "Maybe they'll have a time guessing which body is in the fire. All right, which way do we go?"

Shorty dashed for the shadows from which he had emerged, McCall right at his heels. They avoided a second prone figure and cut back through a narrow passage which flanked a long shed. By that time there was a first class uproar around the calaboose. The cry of "fire" was distinguishable in the din and McCall found himself grinning a little as he ran. He wasn't out of the frying pan yet but somebody else was in the fire. That might help a little, even if it did happen to be a rather gruesome thought.

Shorty slackened the pace when they were skirting the railroad yards. "Looks like we got clean away," he panted. "The broncs are over beyond the water tank where nobody will be likely to spot 'em."

"What do you mean broncs? Just one's enough. You're not going to stick your neck out by going with me."

"The hell I ain't! Doyle wasn't too easy to satisfy last time and he'll know fer sartain that I been workin' with ye on this shindig. So I might as well trail along and git me a full share o' the fun."

"It won't be fun. We'll be bucking a mighty big gang. I don't know just how many, but there's a lot of 'em."

"So there's a lot of 'em. I'm still goin'."

McCall laughed shortly. "You're a great piece of work, Shorty. All your life you've been worrying about all the calamities that you were expecting to happen— and now you're going out of your way to hunt bigger trouble than you imagined even on your gloomiest days."

"Mebbe I jest got tired o' waitin' fer them blamed troubles to hatch out," the little man chuckled. "This time I kin predict grief and make kinda certain I won't be wrong about it. The broncs oughta be right ahead. Take it easy; somebody might've found 'em while I was gone."

That warning proved to be just another of Shorty's false alarms. The broncs were there and no one appeared to dispute with the fugitives as they mounted and·headed eastward along the railroad line. Behind them the din had increased in intensity even as distance caused it to dwindle in volume, and when they looked back they could see a definite glare of fire.

"Looks like there was enough woodwork in that adobe to make a right smart blaze," McCall observed. "Judging by the sound I'd guess that it covered our retreat in right decent fashion."

"Jest what I was thinkin'. I reckon the first lot o' Doyle's men what arrived there was some puzzled. They musta thought their gunnies had slipped and killed ye inside, then ducked outa sight because the regular plan had gone sour. If we're lucky they won't know fer sure what happened 'til they find Manuel and wake him up." He rode along silently for a full minute before he added, "If they ever do."

"Clipped him kinda hard, eh?"

"Sure. No time to take chances. I didn't want him ruinin' my play. Unless he's got a almighty tough skull he won't be botherin' us no more."

They crossed the tracks only when they were well away from the town, swinging then as though by common consent to head for the climb up the Wapitis. McCall made a final effort to dissuade Shorty from further participation in what promised to be such a deadly game, but the little man was obdurate.

"I'm declarin' myself in," he insisted, "My neck's not worth a hoot in Latigo unless we git this mess straightened out, so I might as well help straighten it. Ye ain't been doin' too dang well without me, ye know."

McCall chuckled at the little man's brisk belligerence. "But who'll take care of the stable for you while you're out in the canyons protecting poor stupid me?"

"I reckon Daisy Knowles will look after things."

"You mean the hotelkeeper's daughter?"

"Sure. She knows I'm likely to be missin' come daylight."

"Where does she fit into this? There was a warning

note with my supper and it probably saved me from blunderin' square into a trap. I figured she wrote it."

"Sure she did. I didn't have time to get the full hang of it, but I got the idee Daisy and somebody else has been plannin' to hornswoggle Doyle's outfit. Anyway, she come a-runnin' over to my stable and told me what the plan was about gettin' ye to walk out into gunfire. She said she'd try to make sure that ye didn't do the wrong thing but that it would be up to me to take care of outside matters."

"Which you did, my reckless friend—and good. In case I never get around to it again I'd better thank you now."

"Don't mention it," Langan said politely. "Always glad to toss in a few licks fer a friend in need. Ye know what the poet says. 'A friend in need is the kind ye mostly have hangin' around.' "

"Back to normal," McCall murmured. "Shorty's quoting in his own remarkable fashion. A man could get awful sick of that."

"Don't git uppity," Langan snapped with fine indignation. "It ain't polite to look a gift horse in the dad-ratted bicuspids!"

"I apologize," McCall told him humbly. "Even an ally with a wild strain of philosophy is better than no ally, I suppose."

16

The exchange of banter seemed to make both of them feel a little easier and McCall spoke again, seriously but without the sense of strain. "What do you know about that man Wells, Shorty? I've got a pretty strong notion that he was on our side, probably tied in with Daisy. At least he knew about her note and was trying to make sure that Zellers didn't know about it. Do you figure we're doing the right thing in leaving him behind? He could be in a nasty pickle by now."

"No use worryin' about it," Langan retorted. "We don't know where to look fer him even if we wanted to git plumb crazy and go back to look. Huntin' trouble may be all right fer a feller if he gits a notion for it, but even a dumb galoot like me oughtn't to hunt it that hard."

"You seem to have all the answers. All right. I'll go along with it."

"I shore enough ain't got all the answers," Shorty retorted. "I don't know what in hell this fracas is all about and I figure it's dang near time ye was tellin' me. I don't mind gittin' caught up in a shootin' scrape, but I'd kinda like to know what the shootin' means. And don't tell me it's rustlers; even I ain't stupid enough to think a rustlin' job would have so many gunnies out to kill a man."

They were well out of the pass before McCall could get his story told and the exchange of ideas on the subject of possible explanations lasted all night. It helped to make the climb seem shorter, but McCall knew that dawn was very near when they reached the cut which led into the Devil's Cockpit.

"Now we have to take it easy," he told Langan. "I don't know where Doyle and his pards have been holed up for the past couple of days but there's a chance that they might be in here somewhere. We can't afford to blunder into them."

"Pull up and take a breather," Langan suggested. "The stars are fadin' a mite over in the east so we'll soon be able to read sign. Half hour, mebbe."

"Better move on until we're just short of the intersection. Then we'll climb off and stretch our legs a bit. Did you pack any grub when you got these broncs ready?"

"I didn't ferget a thing like that. A man can't go far on a empty stomach."

"Good. We'll do another quarter mile and then eat. By that time we'll be able to tell whether there's anybody ahead."

The program went off as planned and dawn found them rested, searching for sign in the rocky canyon. The place had been washed clean by the storm but at one point sand had banked up completely across the trail. No one had moved across that area since McCall and the three lawmen had made their way down to Latigo Pass.

"Easy now," McCall warned. "They didn't come this way but there's bound to be other trails into the rustler canyon that I still don't know about. Keep your gun handy when we round the next bend."

They reconnoitered the rocky little valley with fine care but again there was nothing to show that any of the outlaw crowd had been in the vicinity. McCall promptly led the way into the eastern canyon, stopping only to check on the mailbox. It was as he had left it.

"Here we go," he said grimly. "From now on we're traveling blind. I don't know where this leads or how far it goes but it's the trail they use for stolen beef so it ought to bring us somewhere."

"But ye've got a purty good idee, ain't ye?"

"Like I said awhile ago, I figure it swings south and heads toward Mexico. If this is a smuggler outfit, dabbling in stolen beef as a sideline, then this canyon has to connect with some hidden trail across the border. And that's where we're likely to find the outlaws. The natural thing for them to do is to get across the line now that things have gotten so hot."

"That ain't so good. We'll run into a real pack o' grief if we have to hunt 'em down in Mexico."

McCall laughed shortly. "I don't know how they can make any more trouble south of the line than they've been making north of it. I haven't seen anything but trouble since I got off the train.

"Man is of few days and plumb full o' heck," Shorty said in his best sententious manner. "Let's go find some of it."

For an hour the ride took them through a rocky defile much like the canyon which led to K-Bar. There was no real evidence that anyone had ever passed through it ahead of them, but both men knew better than to interpret that absence of sign too literally. The rain had washed out everything. McCall knew that the rustlers had entered the passage and there had been no openings in the solid walls which might mean an alternate route. Any riders who had come into this canyon must have followed it to its end.

Then they came to another of those freak valleys where the towering rimrock seemed to have collapsed in a tumbled mass of broken rocks and loose shale. It required a lot of scouting to determine the route of the cattle thieves but eventually they found sign along a cliff where a grotesque overhang had prevented the storm from doing its work.

"Looks like the best bet," McCall said, pointing to the blurred marks and motioning ahead toward an opening which led out of the ugly little glen. "This runs on toward the south so it fits my idea of what we want."

"Let's go," Shorty agreed tersely. "I didn't see nothin' that looked like sign nowhere else."

After that the trail followed the bottom of a winding gulch which was more of a rocky draw than a canyon. Gradually it took them downgrade and a little more directly into the south until suddenly they could see the glint of railroad tracks in an opening ahead of them. By that time they seemed to have gotten clear of the storm's freak path and the sign was quite clear. This was a well-traveled trail; a large number of horses, with or without riders, and a fair-sized herd of cattle had passed through here within recent days. McCall had been studying the ground as they worked out of the storm area and felt certain that no one had passed along here on the trail of the cattle thieves except Glennister. It left those Latigo men still to be accounted for but confirmed the fact that this was the rustler trail.

It was the crossing of the railroad line that offered significant food for thought. Close to the spot where the gulch opened upon the long valley which the railroad graders had used the trail disappeared entirely. That was because it led directly to a surface ledge of rock upon which marks did not show.

McCall traced the ledge with his eyes, nodding to Langan as he did so. "Smart operators, our outlaws. They've found a way to cross the railroad so their tracks won't be noticed. See how that rocky strip runs almost to the edge of the track ballast? All they need to do is to wipe out the trail where they make the actual crossing, and then they come out on some more rock where prints won't show. It explains why track workers have never noticed anything out of the way."

"And that ain't all," Langan added. "This here's a mighty convenient short cut fer Doyle and his Latigo boys. Now we know how they meet up with their pards without makin' the long ride we just made."

McCall nodded and they crossed to where the rock ledge ended against a sheer cliff. There they had to separate, searching in either direction on the rocks for the trail which they knew had to be there. It was Langan who found it once more but they could not find any indication that riders from Latigo had ever cut the trail at that point. It was not a matter to delay them, however, and they set off promptly, winding into another rugged valley where there was no difficulty in following the outlaw trace.

Progress was slower now. They had to rest their tiring ponies more frequently as the day wore on and there was

156

an ever increasing need for vigilance. Every mile took them closer to a climax which might mean an end to everything, one way or another.

Only one thing of importance came to their attention. At a point some four or five miles south of the rail line they found a fork in the trail. A second route came in from the right there, merging with the path they were following. Shorty noted it with an exclamation. "Now I kin stop worryin' about that part," he grimaced. "Here's where the Latigo fellers ride in. This has just gotta be a short cut leadin' out to the railroad east of town. I'm glad to git that offa my mind."

"Don't be so happy about it," McCall said dryly. "From now on we've got a double chance of having an enemy closing in behind us."

"And ye talk about me bein' a gloom-catcher! Alongside o' that I'm jest a little ray o' dad-ratted sunshine!"

He watched the back trail anxiously from that point on, however, and they moved ahead cautiously, aware that the force ahead must be a rather formidable one. McCall knew that he had seen at least six or eight men in Latigo who belonged to Doyle's outfit and there had been other rustlers in the canyons. Maybe even more down here south of the line. It wasn't going to be any picnic for two men to cope with such an army.

In spite of the slower pace he felt sure that in mid-afternoon they must have crossed the border into Mexico. Not that the desolate country looked different; it was simply that the border was close to the rail line here and they had come quite a few miles since crossing the tracks. Still there was no sign of a camp anywhere along the trail. Just that well-marked path of horses and cattle.

"It can't be too far ahead," Shorty grunted, shifting wearily in his saddle. "If this crowd is haulin' smuggled stuff outa Mexico it stands to reason they won't have their camps more'n a good day's ride apart. We come a fur piece since we left the Devil's Cockpit. The seat o' my pants is gettin' dang near numb."

"Far enough to make matters pretty dangerous for us," McCall reminded him soberly. "If we make any mistakes down here we won't be in any position to holler for help."

Shorty grinned tiredly. "There ye go again! I thought I was the official calamity howler for this outfit."

"You're the howler, all right," McCall retorted, grinning briefly at the little man's humor. "I mean that literally. If and when we find our quarry your job is to hold back while I try to get a good look at 'em. Then you're to high-tail it for Latigo and howl for help."

"Like hell! I'm goin' with ye."

"You are not! There's no sense in both of us taking the same risk. I'll do the looking while you cover the rear and be ready to ride for help in case I need it. We don't want to be dead heroes; we want to break up a gang of outlaws."

"Rats!" Shorty grumbled. "Fine way to treat a man. I mighta stayed right to home if I'd knowed ye wasn't goin' to cut me in on none o' the fun."

McCall smiled crookedly at the change in the little man's tune. Langan had spent most of his life anticipating imaginary troubles, but suddenly he had found a thirst for real trouble. Larry could only hope that the wild ambition would not prove too easily satisfied.

They covered another mile, conscious that the daylight was beginning to wane and then Shorty broke the silence again. "Look, Larry. Over the rocks ahead, Smoke."

McCall pulled up abruptly, studying the trail and the contours of the ground ahead. "Looks like it's just around the next bend. Probably the camp we've been looking for. This is where I take to the woods while you keep shady and be ready to dig out if anything goes wrong. Don't get ambitious now."

The reply came from an unexpected and entirely unwelcome quarter. Directly at McCall's left a nasal voice barked. "Get them hands up high! Ain't neither one of yuh goin' to git ambitious!"

A single glance warned that there would be no chance of making a break. Two hard-looking men had stepped out of a mesquite clump, both of them holding six-guns leveled. Neither gunman was known to McCall, but he didn't need any introduction. It was all too clear that the outlaw gang had been smartly efficient in organizing their outpost.

"Ride on. Slow," the big man with the nasal voice ordered. "And no funny moves unless yuh want to git daylight let through yuh. We're amblin' along right behind."

Shorty wrinkled his nose dolefully as he darted a sidelong glance at McCall. "Why can't I keep my big mouth shut?" he mourned. "Me, I wanted excitement."

The big man laughed harshly from behind them. "Don't beller, runt. Yuh ain't goin' to stay excited long. We don't keep visitors many hours in this climate. They kinda have a habit o' goin' sour on us."

McCall's face was drawn and tired as he met Shorty's eyes. "Sorry," he said briefly. "I should have been looking for something like this."

The remark brought a jeer from the second of their two captors but McCall scarcely heard it. For the instant his mind had turned to another regret. His fine hopes for a rebuilding of K-Bar could be forgotten now. The trap was complete.

Then he forced the thought away and concentrated on the scene which was coming into view around the bend in the gulch. The old urge to find a way of counter-attack was coming back quickly. He could even grin a little wryly as Langan murmured, "The best laid plans o' mice and men shore git fouled up to a fare-ye-well." Somehow the little man's whimsical comment helped.

The outlaw camp was hidden securely in one of those unexpected glades which seemed so out of place among the rugged mountains which served as a concealment. That it was a permanent hideout was shown by the three shacks which occupied the west side of the little valley and by the two crude but large corrals which were built on the opposite side. For the first time Mc-Call really appreciated the scale of the enterprise he was fighting. This was no small local venture of a few thieves; it was bigger than he had suspected even when he had considered the number of men known to be involved. There were a dozen tough-looking characters in sight, most of them complete strangers to him, and the whole picture indicated organization and efficient backing by someone with money and influence.

A flurry of attention stirred the camp as the prisoners were herded in, and a burly man came to the door of one of the shacks shouting an order to someone by the corrals. Even in the fading light McCall saw that the man was Ears Trondell, the rather mysterious ruffian who had played beef dealer in Latigo and who had tried that first attack outside Langan's stable. It seemed evident that Trondell was the boss here, regardless of what rôle he had played in Latigo Pass.

Behind him came the towering figure of Marshal Ross Doyle while at one of the supper fires a man stood up to stare with perplexed surprise at the newcomers. It seemed clear that Walt Glennister hadn't expected to see Larry McCall so soon again. Maybe that was a good point to keep in mind. If Glennister had not known of McCall's escape from the cellar at K-Bar it seemed certain that no one in this camp would know anything about the more recent events in Latigo Pass.

Trondell shouted instructions for a new set of guards to cover the spot where the trap had been sprung, then he strolled across to meet the prisoners, his grin as amiable as though he were greeting friendly guests. McCall sized him up carefully, remembering that the man had been a rather successful salesman in Latigo Pass. Maybe that would account for his urbane air. It would not be smart to take Trondell's smile too seriously; the man was all the more dangerous for his mask of good humor.

"I sorta thought you'd show up, McCall," he greeted, the grin disclosing a missing tooth in front. "After the fancy jobs you pulled off in town it seemed likely you'd get too smart for your britches. I hope you ain't got too many fellers followin' you; we wouldn't know where to put you all if we have to haul many in."

Larry bowed ironically. "Sorry to be such a nuisance," he assured Trondell, adopting the same sort of polite tone. "I'll be happy to relieve you of the burden at any time."

Trondell guffawed loudly. "You've got your nerve with you, McCall," he agreed, still making a good show of his amusement. "But don't worry about crampin' us none. We always manage to pay off a debt of politeness. I took a nap with you as host, and I'm in duty bound to pay you back. If you know what I mean." He cackled again and this time there was something chilling in the merriment. The missing tooth and the enormous ears made him look like some sort of grotesque buffoon, but McCall had a feeling that Ears Trondell was one of those sadistic creatures whose ready smiles cloak a peculiar deadliness. Ears was the sort of outlaw who would laugh at a man while torturing him to death Indian fashion.

Ross Doyle pushed forward then. "Cut the comedy, Ears. We'll knock a few answers outa these here pilgrims and then git rid of 'em. McCall's made hisself a nuisance fer the last time. And we ain't got no reason to put up with nosey Langan neither."

Trondell's grin faded. "I'm ramrod o' this camp, Doyle," he snapped. "You stay outa this." Then he looked back at McCall, grinning again. "Better climb down, redhead. You too, Shorty. Time you hombres had a rest."

The prisoners dismounted silently, wondering what they might expect next from their overly genial captor. Trondell took a step forward, extending a thick, hairy hand to McCall. "Shake, mister," he invited. "Just to show it's all polite and friendly."

Larry took the hand briefly, not knowing what else to do, and Trondell stepped back again. It was clear that he was enjoying this cat-and-mouse game for he grinned broadly as he ordered, "Now tie 'em up, Jerry! Make it plenty tight."

The job was performed swiftly and roughly while Trondell stood back and chuckled, evidently in high good humor over the chance he had found to display his warped humor. When both men were still erect but tied hand and foot he moved toward McCall again.

"And now for the first payment on that little debt of gratitude I was talkin' about."

McCall saw the blow coming but he was helpless to avoid it. Trondell's big fist swung from his boot tops to crash hard between McCall's eyes. Then the early dusk turned into deepest midnight.

17

When McCall regained his senses he was lying on the ground, still bound and helpless. One man stood beside him but the rest of the group had moved away and were standing or sitting around the fires on which supper was cooking. Shorty Langan was not in sight.

"Goin' to open yer purty little peepers, are yuh?" the outlaw jeered, the familiar nasal tones helping Mc-

Call to gather his wits about him. This was the man who had done most of the talking for the pair who had made the capture.

"Git yerself awake," the fellow continued harshly. "I don't want to stand around here all night—and I ain't fixin' to tote yuh while yuh kin still jump. Git up!" He accented the command with a viciously probing boot toe and McCall rolled clumsily, trying to get himself off the ground before the outlaw could indulge his brutal instincts further.

The man haw-hawed and reached out to haul the prisoner erect. "Now hop toward the fire," he rasped. "The boss wants to ask yuh a few questions while the rest of us eat. Ain't much point in wastin' good grub on yuh."

McCall hopped, the effort making his head ache. Trondell's heavy fist hadn't done him any real good, but he could still think clearly enough to know that he had to obey orders if he wanted to play for time. Twice he went sprawling and each time the nasal voiced man yanked him up and shoved him forward again. By that time most of the other thugs had turned to watch the performance, most of them howling with glee at the mishaps of the helpless prisoner. It seemed evident that Ears Trondell had collected a crew of villains much like himself. Baiting a helpless man seemed to appeal to them hugely.

Only Ross Doyle offered an objection. "Why can't yuh make short work of 'em and git it over, Ears? Yuh'll fool around 'til somethin' happens."

Trondell glowered at him across the fire. "What can happen, you fool? This ain't Latigo Pass where every half-baked pilgrim can make a monkey of the boss."

Several of the men roared at this sally but Doyle did not retreat from his stand. "Go ahead. Make jokes—if that's what yuh call 'em. But don't ferget the federals are onto us somehow. If they had two men in Latigo it stands to reason they got more handy. We ain't got no way o' knowin' how much them polecats reported."

"We're in Mexico, stupid." Trondell grated, dropping all pretense of geniality. "And I'm callin' the play here. Just keep that in mind."

Doyle stepped back and Trondell went into a whispered conference with a couple of outlaws unknown to McCall. It gave Larry a chance to drop to the ground near the fire, thinking swiftly over that remark about federal men. Two of them spotted in Latigo Pass. Did it mean that the gang had disposed of them? Apparently it did, judging by the way the reference had been made. The names of Ott and Jones suggested themselves but there was not time to think about it.

Trondell came across to stare down at the silent McCall. He was grinning again but not with the same pretense of good humor. "Want to talk a bit, McCall? You can make it sociable or not. We got other ways."

"The other ways won't be much worse," McCall told him. "Your sample of sociability didn't exactly appeal to me."

Trondell laughed. "We can get a heap nastier than that. And we will if you don't speak up right sharp. How did you get out of that cellar where Walt dumped you? Did Shorty Langan blunder along and turn you loose?"

"No. Shorty never went near K-Bar. We climbed out through a trap door that even the Tanners didn't know about. I knew it was there because I helped build the cabin." He didn't know why he should resort to so ingenious and useless a lie but it didn't seem right to tell the truth to this outfit if he could avoid it.

In the shadowy background Glennister cursed once but Trondell motioned for silence. "What about the Tanners?" he demanded. "They ain't waitin' for you to come back, are they?"

"Of course not. I told them exactly what I suspected

and explained why Latigo's fine marshal couldn't be asked for help. They're turning in an alarm over at Mesa. Maybe they've even got help on the trail by now."

"Like I told yuh," Doyle burst out. "We better string these hombres up quick and git outa here."

"Yeah," Glennister agreed. "Add the federal man to the pair of 'em and we kin have a right nice lynchin' party for a farewell salute."

"Shut up!" Trondell roared. "You're talkin' like a bunch of damned fools! We don't even know this jigger's tellin' the truth—and if he is we're still outa the reach of anybody they can put on the trail from the Mesa. McCall, what did you do after you left K-Bar? If you got outa that cellar so dam' quick you've had quite a bit of time on your hands—time to meet up with your two-bit partner. Explain yourself."

McCall wondered what sort of yarn Shorty had told but he extemporized quickly. "I went straight to Latigo Pass and got Shorty. Then we cut back and followed the canyon trail. It brought us here."

"Yeah? And nobody stopped you at Latigo?"

"No."

"See anything of a jigger who called hisself Bart Wells?"

"No."

Trondell shook his head angrily. It was clear that he was a little confused. McCall's story sounded true but the outlaw chief couldn't quite understand it. On his part, McCall could only wonder at the reference to Wells.

Suddenly Trondell seemed to make up his mind. "Put him in with Langan and the other jigger. I got to know more about what's goin' on in town before I do anything else. That fool Dangler oughta be gittin' back before long and we'll have more to go on."

"Aw, shoot 'em and git it over," an outlaw growled. "Save the fancy stuff for some other time."

165

"Shut up, all of you!" Trondell snarled. "Dammit, that's why none o' you rannies would ever be anything but fly-by-night gun hands and two-bit rustlers if you didn't have somebody to think for you. No imagination. Suppose we hang these jaspers right off? Where does it get us?"

No one ventured a reply to the furious tirade and Trondell answered his own question. "All we get is a sheriff's posse huntin' us all along the border, maybe even stirrin' up the Rurales on this side. We don't want none o' that. We're goin' to keep these polecats on ice 'til we hear from Latigo. When we know what's what we'll work out a scheme to use 'em for our own special benefit." He relaxed to grin suggestively around the circle. "Me, I like the idea o' havin' a suspect handy when I've got a killin' to do. We've already got two dead men so it oughta be useful to have some suspects on tap. We'll plant these jiggers, dead, where it'll take the pressure off us."

"I get it," Glennister said hastily. "That's why yuh didn't finish off the federal man. These critters are goin' to have accidents happen to 'em plenty far away from where we want the law to be lookin'."

"You're almost smart, Walt," Trondell said sarcastically. "You and Doyle together could make one medium grade halfwit. Now put this pest with the others and make sure they're all tied up plenty tight. We don't want no slips."

McCall was yanked away roughly but he had found time to survey the outlaw company pretty carefully. There were fourteen men in camp, counting the pair who had gone to take over the outpost along the trail. Trondell, Doyle and Glennister he could identify by name and he remembered that the two who had gone to do picket duty had been called Mulligan and Ike. Of the remaining nine, one was a shifty-eyed little fellow whose nervousness seemed to irritate his companions. At any rate, they left him strictly alone. Four of the others were Mexicans and one was a burly Negro. There was not a cutthroat in the crew who would hesitate at anything.

He stored the information away in his mind, unhappily aware that it probably would never do him any good. Then he was hurled into one of the cabins to fall hard and roll against another body.

For some moments there was no sound except the clack of voices outside, but then someone spoke cautiously from the darkness. "Welcome to our city, partner. Light the festive lamps and shake hands all around."

It was a grim voice in spite of the forced humor, but it had a strangely familiar ring to it. McCall rolled to relieve some of the strain on his bound arms before answering and it was Shorty Langan's voice that filled the interval.

"Ain't this a helluva time to be makin' jokes?" the little man inquired. "Is that you, Larry?"

"The same," McCall replied. "Who's the joker?"

"Glad to meet you, McCall," the oddly familiar voice said. "I've already greeted Brother Langan. As for me, I'm Walter Clifford, former pride of the revenue service. As of right now I'm tied up tighter than a growing boy's breeches."

"Me, too," Shorty complained sympathetically.

McCall grunted. "You don't sound like any Walter Clifford to me, mister. You've changed your style of talk but you still sound like a man who's been calling himself Wells. If this is a dodge to get me to talk you might as well give up."

"You've got a sharp ear, my friend. I was Bart Wells as late as mid-morning today. Then I rode into this camp with a lot of bright ideas and ran smack into an old murderer friend of mine. He shot off his mouth and my fine romantic career of disguise ended."

"That makes a good yarn," McCall said, openly skeptical.

167

"But not a happy one because it's unfortunately true. You certainly suspected something in Latigo last night, didn't you? Why did you think I passed that note to you?"

"I was wondering. It could have been a friendly move or it might have been a smart double-cross."

The other man's flippancy left him and his voice was sober as he explained. "It was like this. You might as well believe it, not that it's going to make any difference to either of us. I came to Latigo Pass on a very secret job. I managed to work my way into Doyle's confidence enough so that I got a pretty good idea of what he was doing. Then you happened on the scene and matters started to get rough. Twice I thought I was going to be forced to give my hand away to save your hide but both times you wiggled your own way out. Yesterday morning I got orders from Doyle, by a crook called Ten-spot, telling me to be on hand to act as jailer when the sheriff's deputy would be called away. I don't know how Doyle managed to work it out but everything went as he planned while he stayed out of Latigo to keep his alibi complete. I guess you know what sort of plan was afoot; you had that deputy suspicious enough so that he was making himself pretty plain when he left town. Then you showed that you had your wits about you when the time came for the break to be made."

"It wasn't a hard plot to guess," McCall said shortly. "Where were you when we were having all the excitement at the calaboose?"

"Tied up behind the stinkin'est stable in Latigo Pass. Bein' tied up was part of the plan, to keep me clear of suspicion. At that time, remember, I was still one of Doyle's boys. Putting me back of the stable was Jake Zellers' idea of a good joke."

"Sounds like the brand of humor I'd expect from these thugs. Go on with the yarn."

"Well, it took some little time before Zellers could

168

figure out what had happened at the jail. He was having to be the master mind for the gang with everybody else out of town, and Jake's not well equipped for that kind of a chore. Finally, however, they got the fire out and were able to decide that the body was not yours. By that time somebody had stumbled on the equally deceased body of a Mexican named Manuel. That was enough for even Zellers' brand of intelligence. He hustled over and cut me loose, telling me to ride out here and pass the word to Doyle and Trondell. The directions he gave me seemed like the answer to everything I'd been trying to learn. Too bad I'm not going to get much good out of the knowledge."

McCall passed up the note of gloom. "But you didn't tell Trondell about the Latigo business," he suggested. "They don't seem to know anything about that part."

"No. I was spotted by an old convict acquaintance before I could open my trap, so I refused to talk at all. They knew something must be amiss in Latigo Pass so they sent a rider in to get the story. Now tell me your tale of woe."

McCall told him as briefly as possible, filling in the details of the jailbreak but letting Shorty Langan explain most of the rest of it. Clifford had just snapped a question about the nature of the rustler trail when there was a distant yell and a rattle of hoofbeats.

"That wouldn't be the cavalry coming to rescue a missing revenue man, would it?" McCall grunted, a little wryly.

"It would not," Clifford replied. "I was a lone wolf on this chore. I didn't even tumble that there was another federal man working right at my elbow until he made a wrong move and got himself killed."

"Henderson Ott?" McCall asked.

"Hell, no! Ott was just what he claimed to be, a land agent who was getting too big for his pants. The little fellow who called himself Jones was really a Deputy

United States Marshal. He showed too much interest in the Ott shooting and somebody got suspicious of him. Zellers knocked him off and the gang searched him. He had his papers and a badge on him so they stuck a knife in him."

"So that's how it happened there was a federal officer testifying that I stabbed Jones and put a slug into Ott?" McCall muttered. "I figured it was something like that."

"Right," Clifford told him shortly. "One of the gang posed as Akers long enough to impress that fat sheriff."

"Better knock off the chin music," Langan snapped. "I hear somebody comin'."

The oncoming footsteps halted at the door of the cabin, indicating that a guard had been posted somewhat belatedly. It put a stop to the talk but the uncomfortable prisoners were willing to listen now, all three of them curious about the new arrivals who were just riding into camp. McCall even managed to roll toward a crack in the cabin wall which permitted a faint flicker of firelight to enter the place. He had to prop himself in a rather painful position but by doing so he could hear the voices around the campfire.

It did not take many minutes to learn that the new-comers in camp included Jake Zellers and the man who had ridden to Latigo for news. They were making a big fuss about telling the story of the jail-break and the failure of the ambush, the yarn interrupted only by occassional curses from Ears Trondell.

The outlaw chief had lost all trace of blandness by the time the yarn was complete, swearing reprisals on the prisoners that would have done credit to an Apache. It seemed to leave Zellers in a hesitant mood for his voice was pretty shaky as he passed along his final word.

"The big boss says to go easy on them polecats, Ears," he quavered. "He's got plans."

"Go easy on 'em!" Trondell roared. "I'm goin' to cut 'em up in small bits! I'll . . ."

"The boss says we don't want any marks on 'em," Zellers insisted, still showing uneasiness at having to argue with Trondell. "He figures we got to make it look like the federal man was chasin' McCall and Langan fer the killin' o' the Akers hombre. If we set it up careful so it'll look like they all killed each other, somewhere off on the other side o' the mountains, it'll take all the heat off us and lead any more lawmen away from our real territory."

Trondell subsided quickly. "Dammit, that was my idea in the first place. I just got a bit hot under the collar. All right, we'll touch 'em up in a few spots where it won't show."

There was a dead silence for several minutes and then Trondell snapped another order. "Haul them polecats out here and feed 'em," he barked. "If we gotta keep 'em fer a few days while we get our plans straight we'll have to have 'em in good condition for the show. Also we'll have to tie 'em up different. It won't look right if the corpses show marks of rawhide on their wrists."

McCall rolled swiftly away from his listening post. "They're hauling us out again," he whispered. "Don't be fooled by anything and watch my lead. If I get any kind of a chance at all I'm going to make a play."

"What kind of a play?" Langan asked.

There was no chance to explain. The guard at the door had stepped inside, closely followed by two other outlaws.

18

One of the outlaws was carrying a lantern and the other stepped forward briskly, speaking in a tone which reminded McCall unpleasantly of Trondell. It was remarkable the way these thugs aped the twisted humor of their leader.

"All ready fer supper, gents?" the fellow asked with a malicious grin. "It looks like the boss wants to do yo' all proud. Git up on yore hind laigs and hobble out here. Grub's on and yo're next."

They practically had to carry Clifford, but presently the three prisoners were deposited near the fire and Trondell took over the conversation. Evidently the outlaw chief had decided that he might as well indulge in a little of his peculiar style of prisoner-baiting while he was carrying out the orders of the mysterious big boss.

"Sorry you boys ain't got much longer to have any fun outa life," he said, solemnly apologetic. "No hard feelin's, you know, so we'll keep things as bright and cheerful as we can while your miserable lives go on. Lanky! Untie their hands and let 'em tear into some vittles. Keep the ropes on their ankles, though; no use lettin' 'em get bad ideas. It could be unhealthy."

The men around the circle seemed divided in their attitudes toward this by-play. Some of them were following Trondell's lead in making a ghastly joke of the pre-execution ceremonies, but Doyle and a couple of others were frankly worried. All of them were conspicuously alert, their uneasy hands seldom far from their gun butts.

Trondell did all the talking for quite a while, the prisoners content to take the food that was being handed to them with so much mocking ceremony. It was good to eat again, good to be rid of those torturing ropes. What the future might bring they were willing to forget temporarily.

Finally, Trondell asked a little more crisply, "How about it, McCall? Ready to talk sense for a change?"

"Along what line?"

"We want to know what happened in Latigo Pass last night."

"That's easy. I'll tell you all about it." He did so, going into some detail. Since the outlaws already knew the facts it could do no harm to be frank with them and it might puzzle them a bit to have him suddenly turn truthful. The only point on which he held out was the matter of the warning note which had been passed to him by Daisy.

There were angry murmurs when he told of the deaths of Ten-spot and Manuel but Trondell motioned for silence. "You've been a right busy bunch o' little bees, ain't you?" he smirked. "Well, this time you've got to the end of your rope. Want to hear what we've got all planned for you?"

It suddenly occurred to McCall that Trondell was a type he had met before. The man was a born ham actor. He was talking now because he had an attentive audience. And because he enjoyed being in a position to make someone else suffer.

"We'll listen," McCall told him politely. "But don't expect us to applaud very loud." He was still going through the motions of eating, chiefly because he didn't want the outlaws to retie his hands until it became necessary.

"Thanks," Trondell mocked. "You're so damned nice about it I almost hate to have you killed. Or I would if you didn't have so many damned cussed things about you."

He looked around as though expecting some recognition of his wit and added slowly, "First we're goin' to take you and your half-pint partner back into the canyon close to K-Bar. That's where we'll leave you, fixing things so it'll look like the brave Mister Langan had trailed a killer and shot it out with him, both gents gettin' killed. That'll fit fine with the story we're goin' to promote around Latigo Pass. We'll have it all worked out how a jasper named Wells helped McCall to break jail, killin' Manuel and Ten-spot in the process. Then they stole a hoss from Shorty and he went after 'em. Kinda neat, hey?"

"What about me?" Clifford demanded. "Don't tell me you can't find a part for me in the show."

Trondell grimaced. "You're travelin' a bit first, partner, but you'll have your act. You git planted in a canyon about a hundred miles west of here. That'll make it look like you was interested in that part of the country instead o' this. I don't reckon none o' your friends will connect you with a missin' hombre named Wells."

"Sounds practically airtight," McCall commented. "It seems to let you out all around."

Trondell's malevolent leer was almost a beam and McCall thought again of the ham actor. It was certainly obvious that the big-eared outlaw loved to strut, loved to have an audience for his villainy. Now he nodded pompously toward the two men who had brought the prisoners from the hut. "I reckon our good friends are well enough fed, boys," he announced. "Better take 'em back and tie 'em up while we have a little confab about ways and means o' depositin' the various corpses in just the right spots." His tone took on a deeper tinge of pomposity as he added, "Please see that they ain't too comfortable, but don't kick 'em where it'll show. We don't want no marks on the carcasses."

The outlaws howled with glee and the two guards rose to the occasion as they started to obey orders. The one who had imitated Trondell's humor earlier now made a mocking bow as he stooped to haul McCall to his feet. The movement was his undoing. One of those unbelievably fast hands went into action and the outlaw's gun seemed to fly from its holster, the barrel clipping the startled man behind the ear as it came out and up. He went down like a log, not knowing what had hit him—but his companions knew. They suddenly found themselves menaced by a steady gun which had appeared in McCall's hand without any of them having had time to do a thing about it.

"Don't anybody move!" Larry warned as the laughter died away abruptly. "I'll kill the lot of you before anybody can get me. Ask Zellers."

Evidently they had heard enough about McCall and his speed with a gun. Only two men failed to obey the order. Shorty Langan and Clifford both rolled to get clear of the line of fire, Shorty snatching a gun from Zellers as he made the move. Otherwise there was a faltering, motionless silence in the circle of outlaws. The thugs had been caught flat-footed in the midst of their grim merriment and not one of them wanted to be the first to challenge that menacing gun. They remembered too well what had happened around Latigo Pass.

Both Clifford and Langan used the moment of indecision for their own purposes, the revenue man coming up with a knife while Langan managed to stand up and add the threat of his captured gun to that of McCall.

"Nice work," McCall approved, not taking his eyes from the tight little circle of dark faces before him. "Get yourself a gun, Clifford; then cut us loose. Maybe we've found a weak spot in General Trondell's airtight plan."

Langan grinned as he squinted over his gun. "That's the trouble with airtight plans, mostly. They're likely to be full o' wind—like Trondell."

"Don't brag," McCall warned him. "Look what happened to Ears. Hurry it up, Clifford."

The exchange of calm comment seemed to act as a goad on the man who had refused to be amused by any parts of the earlier by-play. Ross Doyle came out of his sulk to make a play, his rage and evident disgust getting the better of his judgment. He rolled swiftly to free his gun, clawing at it with the same motion that shifted his huge body. The weapon was only halfway out of its holster when McCall's gun boomed. Doyle moaned once

175

in a little sound that seemed inadequate to his immense bulk, then he collapsed and lay still.

"Don't anybody else try it," McCall warned coldly. "I'm in no spot to be merciful. If I shoot, I shoot to kill."

There were three guns covering them now and the outlaws seemed to give up. If any of them had entertained ideas of making a break they gave it up after taking a look at Doyle's body. Only Ears Trondell managed to keep his wits enough to talk. He even managed to retain some of his nasty humor as he murmured, "You're a tough hombre, McCall. Too dam' bad you're honest. You'd have made quite a smuggler."

McCall did not allow himself to be drawn into any diverting talk. "Get me an extra gun, Shorty," he directed. "A forty-five. This one's a forty-four and I want a gun that my own shells will fit."

"I'll collect 'em all," Shorty replied. "Then these boys won't be committin' suicide and ye kin have yer choice."

Clifford joined him in the work, both of them going the rounds to make sure that no outlaw could turn the same trick which McCall had used. By the time they had completed the chore and Langan had slipped an extra gun into the waistband of McCall's pants the prisoners were sullenly quiet, apparently having reconciled themselves to full surrender.

Trondell, however, was still pretending a vast amusement, even though his act was wearing a little thin. "I'm gettin' to like your style more all the time, McCall," he observed. "Too bad I'm goin' to have to kill you."

McCall still ignored him. "String up the guns on some of that rawhide they tied our feet with, Shorty," he called. "We'll take 'em along with us."

"They probably got more guns," Langan growled.

"I suppose so. But the more we take the less lead they'll be able to throw later."

Trondell suddenly switched his tactics. "Let's talk this

over, McCall. We oughta be able to make a deal. You and me ain't really got no call to fight each other. We can deal the revenue man out and fix this thing up all right between us."

McCall grinned. "Now that's a different tune! A minute ago you were going to kill me and now . . . Whoa! Stop it! Don't try . . ."

He interrupted his own shout with a gunshot. One of the Mexicans had tried to come up with a holdout gun while Shorty's back was turned toward him. McCall shot the man through the body and paused long enough to make sure that none of the others would try to take advantage of the diversion. Then he went on, speaking to Trondell as though nothing had happened. "No dice, Ears. You see, you don't have a thing to offer in the way of a deal. We hold all the cards."

"Don't fool yourself," the outlaw chief growled, his smile entirely gone now. "You ain't outa this yet."

"We soon will be," Larry told him. "Now, all of you, lie down flat on your bellies and stretch your hands out above your head where I can see 'em every minute. Go on, hurry! The first man who gets tired of digging his nose into the dirt gets a slug in the back to rest him. You too, Ears. We're old chums and all that sort of thing, but I'm getting just a trifle tired of your style of humor. Belly down!"

"You're makin' a bad mistake, redhead. I still got a few good cards in this deal. You . . ."

"Shut up and lie down!"

Trondell obeyed a part of the order, grumbling as he stretched himself on the ground, "I reckon I ain't goin' to feel so bad about shootin' you after all, McCall."

"Got the guns, Shorty? Fine. Now round up seven good broncs. Two apiece so we'll be able to change mounts, and an extra one to carry our nice gun collection. Then shoo all the other ponies out of the corrals. Cut the picket ropes of any you find anywhere else.

We'll make life as miserable for these gents as possible."

"Make it eight horses, Langan," the revenue man cut in. "I've got a nice bit of evidence I'd like to take out of here with me."

"Eight horses it is," McCall agreed. "And hustle it up. These gents are apt to get restless and then I'll have to shoot a few more. Not that it wouldn't be a plumb good idea."

"Go ahead; get cocky," Trondell growled from the dirt. "I'll make you a bet you don't get outa here alive."

McCall recognized the confidence in the fellow's tone. It seemed likely that the outlaw leader had more men close at hand as well as more guns. The retreat was not going to be an easy task, particularly when it had to be conducted in darkness. Still he kept his own words nonchalant as he replied, "No bet, Ears. The winner couldn't collect either way."

Langan and Clifford were working rapidly but the delay was a period of real tension for McCall. It was not easy to keep an eye on so many desperate men, even when they were prone, and he didn't want to do any more shooting if he could help it. Those shots might already have stirred up trouble.

Suddenly Trondell seemed to change his tactics. "Better think it over about a deal, McCall," he persisted, something almost like pleading in his voice. "We let you and Langan get clear away. You leave the federal man to us."

McCall did not relax his watchfulness. "No dice, Ears. In the first place I wouldn't trust you on any kind of deal. In the second place I need Clifford. He's the man who can tell the world all about you and your gang. He's the lad who's going to be my defense against that crooked murder charge you fellows tried to hang on me. If you want to deal, though, I'll make an offer. Name the jigger who shot Henderson Ott and stabbed the other federal man. I'll credit it to your account when you're tried for the murders."

"Now you're talkin' like a dam' fool," Trondell snarled.

"Maybe I'm not. Let's try Jake Zellers on it. Jake, stand up and turn around this way. None of the rest of you make a move!"

He watched alertly as Zellers climbed to his feet to stand glowering ·in the firelight. Then he said slowly, "Jake, you were the big strong-arm man in Latigo. You carried out Ross Doyle's orders when you didn't blunder too much. How would you like to ride along with us and be the fall-guy for this whole stinkin' gang? It wouldn't be too hard to pin everything on you, I imagine. Any jury of Latigo people would think it seemed likely."

Zellers seemed to see the logic of the suggestion. In spite of Trondell's warning curse he whined, "I didn't have a thing to do with it. It was Ten-spot who killed Ott. I dunno who stuck the knife in the federal man. Mebbe Manuel."

McCall had a hunch that the man was lying about the latter part. "Maybe we could find out," he suggested calmly. "Who was it passed himself off as the dead man to Sheriff Brodheiser? Who pretended to be Akers long enough to try pinning the killings on me?"

Panic showed in Jake's grimy features. "It wasn't me, I tell yuh."

"Who was it?" McCall was grimly persistent. He knew that it could not have been Zellers; the false deputy must have been a relative stranger to have played such a game. But this seemed like a good time to force the information to the surface. "It's you or him, Jake. Better talk."

"All right. Lafe Purdy was the jasper what done it. That one right next to Doyle's body." He pointed across toward the far side of the fire.

McCall watched as the man in question began to

squirm. "Over here, Clifford," he called. "Let Shorty finish that chore."

There was an uneasy rumble from the men on the ground but he silenced them with a sharp command, waiting until the revenue agent had returned to the fire. Then he motioned to Purdy and said, "Want to take a look through that jasper's pockets, Clifford? If he's got a badge and some papers I reckon we've caught ourselves the murderer of your friend Akers."

Clifford stepped in and grasped the cringing Purdy by the collar. Hauling him erect he made a quick but efficient search, turning up a card case and a small badge. "Our man, McCall," he said shortly. "I'll have Langan bring an extra pony."

Before he could shout instructions to the little stableman, however, there was an alarming interruption. Something like a thud sounded close at hand while close on the heels of the noise two guns banged from the south edge of the little glade. McCall could feel the wind of a slug whining past his ear, and as he went into a hasty crouch he could see that Purdy was crumpling into the edge of the fire. A shout from Langan indicated that help was on its way but for a split second McCall had to watch everything. Clifford had ducked promptly out of the circle of fire.

Then he realized that there must have been guards posted on the camp's southern approaches. They had heard the shots and had slipped in to find the prisoners in command. Fortunately their sniping shots had injured no one except the outlaw Purdy. There was an uneasy stir among the men on the ground but McCall did not let himself be diverted by the attack. He could not return the fire of men he could not see so he shifted his position, barking an order for Zellers to lie down again. Somehow he would have to keep the situation under control until Shorty could bring up the horses. Otherwise the flight would be ended before it could even begin.

19

There was a momentary lull and then gunfire seemed to break out in a variety of places. Clifford and Shorty were counter-attacking the outlaw pickets and McCall fired two fast shots on his own account, one at an outlaw who had come up with a knife and the other to knock a hideout derringer out of Trondell's beefy fist.

"I'm still running this show!" he snapped, ignoring the bullet that screamed past his head and keeping his attention on the antics of the cursing Trondell. Evidently the slug had knocked the derringer out of the man's hand without actually touching flesh and Trondell was wringing the hand as though it stung plenty. "Keep down and keep quiet or Doyle and Purdy won't be the only corpses around here. Jake! Do you want to ride along with us now that Purdy's dead? I reckon you'll be able to save yourself with a straight story."

"Yuh kin go to hell," Zellers growled, taking courage once more. "I ain't squealin'—and yuh ain't goin' to git away alive!"

A flurry of departing hooves indicated that Langan and the revenue man had driven off the attacking outposts and were once more able to go on with preparations for leaving. McCall yelled quick instructions to them as they came into the circle of firelight. "Leave one bronc beside me, then hold your guns on these hombres while I mount. After I'm in the saddle you two start up the valley. Find the trail and give a yell. Then you can cover me while I come along."

He mounted quickly and added for the benefit of the

silent outlaws, "You fellows heard that. Don't try anything or there will be some more lead coming your way. If you're real smart you won't make any fool plays. Ready, Shorty? Clifford?"

The revenue man was leading a pony which carried a bulky pack. One of the other spare horses was decorated with captured outlaw guns and cartridge belts so Larry decided that Clifford was taking along some evidence of the smuggling ring. Even more than before he realized that the Government man was his only real hope for getting himself a clear slate with the law. No one else could do so much to prove that he had not been guilty of those Latigo Pass murders. This was not going to be a mere retreat; he had to make sure that the revenue man got clear away with that bronc-load of evidence. Under the circumstances it might turn out to be a tough problem.

The first stages of the retreat went off without a hitch but as they began to feel their way along the dark trail to the north they could hear Trondell bellowing angry orders behind them. It was a safe bet that pursuit would be prompt. The outlaw roost certainly boasted some kind of armory where their men could be rearmed and the smuggler crowd would be desperate to stop the men who threatened their very existence.

Shorty took the lead, seeming to possess cat's eyes in the inky blackness as he found the winding trail. McCall brought up the rear, riding in complete silence until he had checked both of his guns and made certain that they were reloaded. Then he asked, "Did either of you get hurt in that skirmish?"

Both men reassured him and Clifford asked, "Where are we, do you know?"

"Not exactly. I figured we were somewhere in Mexico. Not many miles south of the line."

The revenue man grumbled ruefully, "Can't you make another guess? If we're on Mexican soil I'm not only violating my orders about observing the international boundary, but I'll actually be the one who's running dope into the United States."

"Dope?" Langan barked. "Is that what ye got loaded on that bronc?"

"That's it. Mostly opium. We've been a long time locating the leak but we knew that considerable quantities of the stuff was coming through. I stumbled on what looked like a hot clue and came to Latigo Pass."

"But you had the Apache mining outfit as your number one suspect, didn't you?" McCall put in.

"How do you know that?"

"Because that's where I fell into the game. Apache got worried because they knew somebody was mighty interested in their mine wagons and ore shipments. They were afraid it meant some kind of hijacking plan on the fire; they never even guessed that they were being spied on by revenue men because they were suspected of smuggling dope."

"Sounds like you know most of the yarn."

"It's all pretty clear now. Were you and Akers working together?"

"Not at first. I didn't even know another man was on the same job but then I caught onto him. We had time for just one search of the mine wagons in a fake holdup and then he tipped his hand to the Latigo gang. Lucky for me you came along."

"Think nothing of it," McCall told him dryly. "I'm planning to get my money's worth out of you if we get clear. I'll need a good witness to prove that I'm not a killer."

"I'm your man—and glad to do it."

"Fine. Then I'll make another guess at our location. I must have been all wrong a few minutes ago. We're on United States soil."

Clifford laughed aloud. "That's decent of you. Now forget the official story and tell me where we really are.

I came in at night, using a trail that left me pretty much confused."

McCall explained as clearly as possible, describing the country ahead and the relative location of Latigo Pass. The revenue man grunted briefly and suggested, "We'd better head west along the railroad if we miss the short cut in the dark. I'll guarantee your safety when we hit town."

"That's what I had in mind. The only point that bothers me is the short cut, the one you must have traveled. I'm not sure we can find it in the dark. If we miss it and ride on into the canyon country this side of the track there's a chance that our friends will be able to outflank us. After all, they know the country and we don't."

Clifford did not reply and they rode on in silence for some minutes. Once there was the sound of a distant shout behind them but they could not hear anything which indicated serious pursuit. The fact was more alarming than anything else. There could be only one reason for the outlaw failure to give quick chase. The outlaws had a better plan.

The night ride became a nerve-wracking affair of slow progress and tense delays. Twice they lost the trail entirely and were lucky to find it again. Always they had to ride along in silence, momentarily expecting the worst. Speed was out of the question and it was maddening to continue the slow pace when it was growing so clear that the smuggler crowd must be up to some sort of smart strategy.

"This thinkin's gettin' me wore raw between the ears," Shorty Langan complained after some three hours of it. "I was all set to shoot my way out, but this sneaky business ain't healthy. What in hell do ye reckon the polecats are up to?"

"Nothing we'll like," McCall told him. "Just keep going and don't get lost any more. We'll find out soon enough."

When the first gray appeared above the eastern hills they halted to switch their saddles to fresh ponies. Daylight would surely bring some sort of crisis and they wanted to be well mounted when the showdown came. McCall had hoped that they might find the short cut to Latigo Pass, but it was evident that they had missed it in the darkness. Now they would have to try the rail line.

"I wonder if we couldn't hole up along the railroad and wait for a train," Clifford suggested. "If we could manage to stop the morning westbound we'd be doing ourselves a right smart favor."

"If we didn't git shot fer train bandits," Langan grumbled. "It's gittin' so nothin' works out right any more."

McCall grimaced at the way the little man was slipping back into his old pessimism. As it turned out they had no chance to try the revenue man's proposals. Progress had been so slow during the night that they were a good half mile short of the railroad when the morning train thundered past. The sound served to give them their bearings and McCall spurred forward, turning his led horses over to Langan. "I'll go ahead and scout," he explained. "If Trondell and his rannies took a good short cut they might have been able to ride around us. We don't want to bust out into any kind of trap."

The long valley was bright with morning sunshine when he reached the rock ledge where the outlaw trail was so carefully concealed. He edged cautiously into the open and halted abruptly at sight of seven riders galloping toward him from the direction of Latigo Pass. A second look told him that one of the men was Ears Trondell. Evidently the outlaw strategy had been exactly as he had called it.

He wheeled his pony promptly and galloped back to meet his companions. "Jump those nags!" he yelled. "We called the turn on that flanking job but we've still got time to get across into the far canyon. If we stay here they'll have us pinched between two forces."

He added a final injunction as the three of them pounded forward toward the escape route which the outlaws were trying to close. "Don't bother to shoot at 'em. They're facing the sun. That's how come they didn't see me. Just get across!"

He led the way into the railroad cut, uneasily aware of the nearness of the oncoming gunmen. Still that slanting sunlight was in his favor and they were actually across the rail line before an opening shot indicated that they had been spotted. After that the lead flew viciously around them but they did not pause to return the fire.

"Three of 'em got rifles," Shorty howled, bending low on his bronc's neck as he drove the animal to practically drag the extra horses.

"Can't we make a stand after we reach cover?" Clifford shouted to McCall.

"No. They'd get behind us. Wait 'til we reach the rock country."

He swung aside to let his companions pass. "Keep going as hard as the broncs will take you. I'll let 'em know we still feel ambitious."

Clifford nodded a little grudgingly but did not slacken his pace. McCall pulled in at the edge of the trees and steadied his gun hand. A show of force right here might delay the pursuit for valuable minutes.

Two riders swung into the gap almost immediately, the big Negro and one of the Mexicans. McCall fired grimly, deliberately, knocking the Mexican from his saddle with the first shot. It took two more slugs to down the other man and by that time bullets were crashing into the trees all around the lone defender. Larry emptied his gun, saw the outlaw charge flatten out and turn into a retreat, then he whirled to ride hard on the trail of his companions. That ought to slow the enemy up a bit—and it certainly shortened the odds.

Even as he spurred forward he was calculating the number that still had to be faced. There had been twelve men in the outlaw camp at one time. With the four extra guards and Zellers they must have numbered at least seventeen. With six dead or badly wounded it left a probable eleven to meet. That was still not a very even fight, but it was better than being tied up and helpless.

He overtook Clifford and Langan within a half-mile, reporting his success briefly. The revenue man grinned with something like the dry humor he had displayed back there in the cabin. "That's the stuff to feed 'em," he approved. "Excellent diet for outlaws, I'd say. As soon as we find a suitable spot we'll let one man ride on with the horses while the other two lay an ambush. Not too soon, though. Give our friends a chance to get careless again."

Twenty minutes passed before they put the plan into execution. Langan drew the job of riding ahead while the other two set the trap at a sharp bend where they could keep their ponies under cover. Once more there was a sharp brush from which the pursuers recoiled after losing one man and having two others wounded. Clifford was inclined to be jaunty over the success of the stand but McCall shook his head grimly as he reloaded. "That stunt won't work again. The minute they draw fire from us they'll have those riflemen fanning out to put a crossfire on us. We've got to ride hard now and keep riding."

The canyon had seemed long when they came down it from the Devil's Cockpit, but now it seemed endless. After another two miles of riding there was a constant skirmishing going on. The outlaws were pressing harder every minute, taking advantage of every straight section of canyon to use their rifles.

Still there were no casualties on either side, the range being entirely too great for saddle shots at moving targets. It was scant consolation and McCall knew that he was growing tense under the strain of the running fight.

Sooner or later an outlaw bullet would make a lucky hit and then they would have to gamble on a real stand against odds.

The thought brought realization of another complication. Where was Sheriff Brodheiser?

With sudden clarity McCall understood the enemy's probable strategy. A messenger to Latigo would soon have a posse riding into the Wapitis, a posse primed to believe that McCall and Langan were fugitive killers. It would prove mighty awkward to run headlong into such a quick-trigger company while engaged in a running fight with the outlaws. It wasn't likely that there would be time for explanations.

Then Clifford's bronc began to go lame. Shorty noticed the fact although the revenue man had said nothing about it. "Time to make another stand," the little man announced calmly, the usual gloom conspicuously absent from his tones. "He who stops and fights a bit will live again to git up and git."

"Poetry with the philosophy now, eh?" McCall chuckled. "Pick the spot, General. We'll hole up and hold the critters awhile so Cliff can ride on and change his saddle to another bronc."

An abrupt bend offered another likely spot and Shorty gave the signal, waving Clifford on. "Hustle it up, mister," he urged. "We won't have no cinch this time. They'll be lookin' for it. We'll give ye ten minutes. No more."

They took positions in much the same manner as before, McCall muttering a brief warning as they picked their vantage points. "Let 'em get close but don't miss a shot—and pick the riflemen if possible. They're the boys who can ruin us."

He was expecting a determined charge by the whole outlaw force or an attempt to do battle at long range. In either case the outlaws would have an advantage, either by mere weight of numbers or through superior weapons. To his surprise only four men appeared in the gulch behind them, four men who rode forward slowly and cautiously. Ears Trondell was conspicuously missing.

"What the hell!" Shorty muttered. "Looks like somethin' different is due to happen."

McCall did not reply but he did not like the looks of the situation any better than Langan did. The four outlaws stopped just out of six-gun range, conferring among themselves before approaching the bend. For some reason they did not seem to be in any hurry. Ten minutes earlier the whole crew had been riding hard, but now there were only four pursuers, two of them wounded, and they were deliberately hanging back. The implication was ominous. The other five or six who were still in real fighting trim must be executing another flanker while these four encouraged the quarry to slow down.

The allotted ten minutes dragged by and still the four did not venture forward. Finally Shorty swore aloud and fired three shots almost blindly in the general direction of the idle horsemen. None of the slugs seemed to do any damage but the four outlaws promptly turned and galloped away.

McCall ran for his bronc at once. "We've got to make tracks," he snapped. "They're circling us again."

They explained it to Clifford as they overtook him, all three driving their mounts hard as they pressed through a narrow canyon which looked a little familiar to McCall. Once before they had managed to elude a trap; maybe they could do it again. In any event it was a real race from now on. Only when the enemy forces were all behind them again could they plan on the stand which would have to be made.

It was shortly past noon when they broke out into the Devil's Cockpit. Clifford was still in the lead and he let out a yell as he cleared the mouth of the canyon.

"Here they come, McCall! From the right. Which way do I go?"

McCall made his decision even before he had ridden into position to see the outlaws bearing down upon them from the K-Bar canyon. Evidently there must be some kind of path across the crags which had permitted Trondell and his men to circle into that other canyon. Now they were driving down it, trying to bottle the fugitives in the rustler canyon.

"Hard to the left and across the opening," he shouted at Clifford. "There's another opening just across there. It leads down the mountains to Latigo Pass. We'll just have to hope we don't get tied up between two parties there."

Neither of the other men offered any objection, and they put spurs to their tired mounts even as the riders in the north canyon began to fire. This was going to be a tight fit, McCall knew. Crossing the Devil's Cockpit under fire was going to take some hard riding and a lot of good luck.

20

"Get rid of those extra broncs," McCall yelled, slashing at a lead rope. Extra horses could no longer be of use. Speed would be everything from now on until they were across the rocky opening.

Shorty obeyed the order but Clifford merely hunched lower in his saddle and spurred his weary mount. He could not cut the spare pony loose without abandoning the animal which carried the evidence. McCall understood and swung past him, prodding the horses into a faster pace. Then he cut away again, drawing the outlaw fire away from Clifford. Langan followed his example, both men firing steadily in an effort to slow down the charge of Trondell's thugs.

A bullet raked across McCall's thigh but he paid scant attention. He knew that he was still gripping his mount with the wounded leg, so the injury could be no more than a scratch. Another slug clipped his hat brim but he had the satisfaction of seeing one of the enemy go tumbling to the rocks.

He changed guns, emptying the second one just as he followed Langan and Clifford behind the first turn of rock in the Latigo canyon. Then, as he quickly reloaded, he knew that the pursuit had slackened. The outlaws had already learned a hard lesson and they were not going to run into another ambush.

"Anybody hurt?" Langan shouted above the clatter of hooves. "I lost a boot heel and got a hunk knocked outa one o' my taps, but I ain't sheddin' no blood."

McCall remembered his own wound and glanced down to see that his levis were showing a lot of red. He stuffed a bandanna down inside the waistband as a compress and shouted a cheerful negative. Only when the makeshift bandage was in place did he realize that Clifford had not replied to Shorty's query.

"Are you hit?" he asked, closing in on the revenue man.

Clifford grinned a little shakily. "Flea bite along the ribs," he admitted. "I'll be all right."

The blood on the side of his shirt belied the words. The man was bleeding quite badly. He would have to have attention before long.

"Take the rear, Shorty," McCall ordered. "Don't fire unless they start to gain on us too fast. We'll make a stand in about a mile. There's a place at the end of this gorge where we can fort up. Do you think you can hold out for a mile, Clifford?"

"What if I don't?" the wounded man grimaced. "You boys go on—but take the dope with you."

"Not on your life!" McCall retorted. "You're our evidence, remember? We're as anxious to get you back as you are to drag in that pack of drugs."

"All right. I'm good for a mile, I reckon. Let's ride."

They drove their mounts hard, avoiding any further skirmishing until they were out of the gorge and on the upper slopes of the Wapiti climb. It was then that they saw the main force of outlaws behind them, Trondell's group as well as the four who had played the cagey game in the south canyon.

McCall motioned toward a rocky crag which stood like a sentinel above the long trail up from the mesquite flats. "Up there," he said briefly. "The broncs can make it, I hope."

There was a treacherous path up one side of the granite pinnacle but otherwise the place seemed completely inaccessible. Once at the summit they could hold out for many hours.

"We'll have to hop to it," Langan grumbled, sliding out of the saddle to lead his horse on the rocky trail. "It'll git mighty awkward if them riflemen start heavin' lead at us while we're makin' the climb. I ain't anxious to be no sittin' duck in no dad-ratted shootin' gallery."

He reached the peak with remarkable agility, then slid back down to help the tottering revenue man to safety. Clifford was wobbling badly but he kept a grim hold on the lead rope of the pack horse, holding hard to his saddle horn with the other hand. McCall brought up the rear, throwing a pair of shots down the trail in an effort to discourage the oncoming outlaws.

They were almost at the top when the outlaws saw the opportunity Langan had warned against. Instantly three men dismounted and began to snipe at the fugitives. Rifle slugs whined from the bare rocks but the only casualty was the horse that carried the precious evidence. The animal staggered and almost fell, but then the climb was over and the hard-pressed men were panting behind natural ramparts of rock.

McCall issued prompt instructions for the defense. Clifford was helped from his saddle and Langan hurried the horses back away from the approaches. By that time the wounded pack animal was sagging so badly that Langan promptly shot him and left him to anchor the others. Then he hurried back to where McCall was working on Clifford.

"We'll be all right," Larry told him. "Hold the top of the trail 'til we get ourselves plugged up and then we'll both be able to help." .

Shorty grimaced as he noticed McCall's wound, but he did as he was told. He crawled to a position near the head of the ascent and almost at once his gun barked three times in·quick succession.

"Need any help?" McCall asked, as answering shots sounded from below.

"Nope. They was dumb enough to try and climb right up here. Like shootin' fish in a barrel. I got two and the rest of 'em hauled their freight pronto."

"Is there any other way for them to get up here?" Clifford asked faintly.

"None that I know of," McCall replied. "I'll look it over better pretty soon. You lie still and get your gimp back. We'll call if we need you."

He crossed to Shorty's side and peered out into the valley below. A rifle bullet made him duck back, but he saw that the outlaws had abandoned the attempt to scale the peak. They were milling around down there on the trail, showing signs of confusion.

"Any water?" he asked Langan.

"Yep. But I plumb forgot to raid the chuck wagon. No grub at all."

"That's bad. I'm tired, empty, thirsty and sleepy. Aside from that and a sore leg I feel fine. Better take the Government man a drink. I'll watch here."

Another quick look over the rim told him that Trondell had bullied his survivors into some semblance of order. Now they were listening to his harangue with evident signs of sullenness. McCall counted only seven riders down there so he judged that Shorty had not over-reported his own success. However, as he watched, one of the outlaws swung his mount and headed down the trail to Latigo Pass. If Trondell had any more men available they would soon join the siege.

Langan returned quickly, his narrow features haggard as he passed the canteen over to McCall. For the first time since the opening of the battle he was wearing an air of concern that was obviously real. "That feller ain't so good," he muttered. "Couldn't hardly hold the bottle to drink. He sure can't ride no more fer quite a spell."

"Neither can I," McCall said tersely. "Anyway there can't be more than a couple of hours of daylight left. We'll stay right here for the night."

"I don't know if he'll make out."

"He isn't bleeding badly, is he?"

"No."

"Then he'll get along. The wound's not too bad; it's just that he's been through so much. By morning he'll be able to stick on a horse."

"But what happens if they try to rush us in the dark?"

"Can you think of a place where we'll be able to defend ourselves any better?"

Suddenly the little man grinned. "Mebbe ye're right," he chuckled. Then he shuffled toward the rim and collected as big a boulder as he could carry. Without a word he rolled it to the top of the climb and went back for another. For a good hour he worked, bringing loose rocks to the head of the steep ascent, and in that time he panted only one grim comment. "We'll make it plenty tough fer any polecats what try to climb up here this evenin'."

McCall was content to conserve his strength, rolling

a cigarette now and then but otherwise remaining perfectly still with an ear cocked for sounds of trouble from below. Dusk came all too soon and then the watchers edged closer to the top of the incline, Shorty arranging his rocks like a battery commander sighting his pet guns. It seemed like a good bet that Trondell would send his men to the attack as soon as the light grew bad for shooting but while they could still see to climb.

A sound behind him gave McCall a start and he dropped a half-smoked cigarette hastily, his quick movement sending the pain afresh through his wounded thigh. Then he relaxed as he saw that it was Clifford who had dragged himself to the rim.

"Make room," a slightly tremulous voice insisted. "I'm good enough to have a hand in this. Are they coming up?"

McCall choked back the protest he had been about to make. An extra gun might come in handy before long.

They did not have long to wait. The clink of a spur on rock far below warned them that action was imminent even though their survey of the valley disclosed nothing but deepening shadows. It was almost dark down there. Then a rock tumbled down from an unseen ledge and they knew that the outlaws were indeed on their way up.

Tense as he was McCall knew a swift admiration for Trondell and his gang. The outlaws were determined rascals, and they had plenty of nerve, especially now since the fight had become a matter of real desperation. Trondell's men knew that their lives would not be worth much if the men on the heights were permitted to get away with their damaging evidence. Consequently they were willing to run grave risks. It was a case of everything to gain and not much to lose.

There were no further sounds from below and after a long listening period McCall became restless. What were the attackers trying to do now? Surely some of them would have had time to reach the summit. He edged forward a little to get a better look and was greeted by the blast of a gunshot from directly below him. Two shadows moved silently there, both of them opening fire. The outlaws had played it foxy; they had climbed the rocks barefooted to avoid noise.

He fired deliberately and knew that the man who had opened the skirmish was tumbling down the slope. Then he blasted a second shot at a moving shadow, conscious all the while that Langan and Clifford were firing steadily. Slugs from below whined past him but he knew that the enemy was firing blindly, doing no damage at all.

For about fifteen seconds there was a regular nightmare of gun flashes and noise. Then the outlaw fire faded out, only a pair of guns booming from just below the rim. At the same time Shorty Langan traded his sixgun for boulders.

It left the little man exposed more than McCall had been, so the other defenders put up a brisk covering fire for him. Shorty rolled rocks feverishly, swearing strange oaths as he worked. Once a man screamed in pain but then the shooting died away entirely and the mountain echoed only to the rumble and clatter of bouncing rocks. Presently even that ceased, the only sound being that of a man's voice raised in painful imprecation to the accompaniment of the last dribble of shale loosened by the Langan artillery.

"We win that round, all right," Clifford said, a little more steadily. "Anybody stop anything?"

Apparently no one had. The defense had not permitted the outlaws to get in a position to shoot accurately. Only Shorty seemed disgruntled. "Doggone it," he complained. "Now I got to git me some more rocks —and I don't even have the fun o' knowin' how the score stands."

"Don't worry about it," McCall advised him. "We're

holding cards, spades and big casino now. We've got the position. And I'd guess that we're not outnumbered any longer."

They divided watches informally, one man staying on the alert until he could no longer keep awake, then arousing someone else to take over. None of them heard any sound from the enemy through the long night, and finally it was McCall who watched the sky growing pale in the east. He had been awake for quite a long time, his wound aching pretty badly as general weariness gripped him. Today would mean another stern test. He and Clifford would have to hold the fort while Shorty made some attempt to get help. If the day should turn hot they would be in a bad position up here on the crag, but the risk had to be taken. Heat and thirst would be better than outlaw bullets.

He tried to shift his position and discovered that the wounded leg had stiffened into painful uselessness. Clifford would be as bad or worse after the night. Neither of them could hope to put through the day without danger of developing fever. Maybe Shorty should make the attempt at getting through before daylight could come.

The dull thought snapped as a boot heel scraped nearby. McCall rolled, taking a sharp jab of pain from the wound, and was dismayed to see Trondell and another outlaw coming over the rim behind him. Apparently they had found another way of scaling the rocky spire.

His gun moved in a desperate burst of speed. There was no question about beating the enemy to the draw this time. The enemy was already aiming.

Still it was practically a dead heat. McCall's gun bucked against his palm just as a stab of pain went through his upper body. It sickened him but he fought the nausea long enough to draw fine on the second outlaw. At the same time he knew that another gun was slamming nearby while a faint echo of the sound seemed to come from far away.

After that he felt himself to be living in a curiously dim void where sounds came clearly enough but where he had no power to move or to speak. He was lying flat, listening to the frantic tones of Shorty Langan.

"He's hit hard, Clifford. See if ye can't edge over to him and help him a bit. I've got to see who's shootin' down there. Sounds like Ears got a new gang o' recruits durin' the night. Got to hold 'em off."

Ears Trondell! In his oddly detached thoughts McCall repeated the name, knowing a queer feeling of peace as he looked at the motionless figure of the outlaw leader. Trondell was finished. So was the other man. Maybe Larry McCall was done, too, but that fast show gun had done its final chore. Too bad a man couldn't . . .

He realized that Clifford was fumbling at a numbed shoulder and he tried to speak, tried to tell the revenue man to stop irritating his own injuries. The words would not come, however, and then he heard Langan's yelp of pleased surprise. "That ain't help fer the gang, boys! Yeow! They got that rustler in handcuffs. They're here to help us. Hey, down there!"

Something in McCall's weary brain seemed to relax. He did not need to fight the blackness any longer. Help was at hand.

When he opened his eyes again he was lying on the ground in a canyon where the afternoon sun did not quite strike. For several minutes he found himself battling with that same dim mistiness of borderline consciousness which had preceded the dark. He could not summon his faculties for action or speech but he was able to hear the talk around him. Mostly he was interested in the voice of a strange man whose broad back was turned toward him.

"Everything must have happened at once in Latigo Pass," the man was saying. "When I got off the train and asked for the mayor I nearly got myself lynched before I could convince the vigilantes that I was not a partner of their former crooked official. Then they gave me the whole yarn."

"But how did you know about Latigo Pass?" Clifford's voice inquired. "Did the main office get itchy about me?"

The newcomer chuckled. "A girl named Daisy something-or-other sent us a wire. It seems she got worried and decided to play her hunch that you were a federal agent in disguise. A smart young lady, I'd say. However, the case had blown sky high before I got to Latigo."

The heavier tones of Sheriff Brodheiser broke in then, somewhat ruefully. "Mayor Estler and his boys pulled a smart dodge in decoying me away from town, but they overreached themselves a bit. I managed to trap one of the rannies they'd set to watch me and he turned out to be a purty famous horse thief. He got scared and talked, tryin' to save hisself. By the time I got back to Latigo Pass I knew all about a dope smugglin' ring that used cattle rustlin' as a sideline for their return trips. I also knew that the town officials of Latigo Pass had made a big show of runnin' a law-abidin' town because it was the perfect screen for 'em. I even knew that Estler ordered the killin' of Henderson Ott because Ott was gettin' to be a dangerous rival for town control."

"And by the time the sheriff hit town he had a gang of folks ready to take his lead. They'd picked up some ideas on their own account when that rancher busted into Latigo and told his story."

"What rancher?"

"Fellow named Tanner. He and his daughter popped into town with a yarn which seemed to fit the facts, but which didn't agree with what Estler was telling. I guess the mayor had got all tangled up when his communications began to bog down. Anyway, there was a vigilante crowd all organized, with Estler under guard when Sheriff Brodheiser arrived with the evidence. At about the same time Stallcup, the mine manager, began to get replies from some wires he'd sent and we began to piece the whole puzzle together. The only problem then was to find out what had happened to you men."

Clifford's murmur of understanding was partly covered by the grate of iron wagon tires on rock. Shorty Langan appeared swiftly, announcing, "They've got the wagons in. I reckon it won't be so hard on our wounded fellers now. How's McCall?"

Suddenly Larry found it possible to answer for himself. "Not bad, Shorty. How long have I been out?"

"Most all day. We brung ye down here where it'd be cooler. Got wagons in to take ye down to Latigo. Kinda spoilin' ye, I reckon, but that's what happens when wimmen git into the deal." He grimaced humorously and added, "They tell me the Tanner gal was as much worried about ye as Daisy was about Clifford. Lucky it wasn't me what got shot up; I'd 'a had to walk in!"

Several voices began to talk at once, everyone trying to assure McCall that his part in the battle was completely understood. He merely grinned, his eyes on the pair of sturdy wagons which were coming around an angle of the canyon. Jim Tanner was driving the first one and a pretty dark-haired girl was on the seat beside him. In the back of his mind McCall knew that the jolting ride to Latigo was going to be a long and painful process, but somehow he didn't think he was going to mind it too much. With a nurse like that on duty a man could take quite a lot.

It was a soberly happy group that camped in the canyon that night. Taking the wagons down over the rocky trail in the darkness was out of the question so McCall and Clifford were made as comfortable as possible in the care of their individual nurses and the brisk little medico who had come out from Latigo Pass. Both men were badly but not dangerously wounded, and McCall was able to get a measure of enjoyment out of the almost dreamy knowledge that the long fight was over and won.

Mostly he was aware of Helen Tanner's solicitous care but the dream was also spotted with bits of conversation that he was to remember later. Once he heard Sheriff Brodheiser's complaint. "This thing woulda been the biggest round-up in the history of the territory if it hadn't been for one thing. There ain't no outlaws but Estler left to arrest."

And then there was the time when the voice of the newly arrived federal man sounded by the side of the wagon. "How's your patient, Miss Tanner?"

"He's resting, thanks," the girl said briefly.

"Good. I guess he's tough enough to come through all right. I hope so, anyway. I'd like to see him give up his private investigations and come over with us. We could use him."

"You won't get him," she replied definitely. "He's going to run K-Bar—with my help."

McCall smiled tiredly. Only through the ragged edge of an overpowering sleepiness did he hear Shorty Langan's complaining chuckle. "That's clear enough, mister. We kin scratch a good man offa the active list. As the poet says, 'A man's a man fer a' that—' 'ceptin' when he gits hooked into bein' a dad-ratted husband!"

Helen's amused laugh was the last sound McCall remembered of the evening. A man could sleep peacefully on such a sound.